Every Witch Way but Flames

Magical Misfits Mysteries – book 10

K.E. O'Connor

K.E. O'Connor Books

EVERY WITCH WAY BUT FLAMES

Copyright © 2023 by K.E. O'Connor

ISBN: 978-1-915378-60-6

Written by: K.E. O'Connor

Chapter 1

Squirrel surprise

This fluffy find wasn't getting away from me. If it took me an hour to drag it to the basement and present it to my wonderful witch, then that's what it would take. I dug in my back paws, clamped my teeth around the squirrel pelt, and pulled. It must have been one heck of a beast when alive. Possibly even larger than me! What a treat.

Why would anyone leave a perfectly serviceable pelt lying around? Well, partially buried under a giant tree. It was the perfect trophy to adorn any wall. I could see it now, pinned to the basement wall opposite the bed, so Zandra would see it every time she opened her eyes. It was the perfect gift.

But it was a heavy gift, and it gave off a pungent odor, especially with my booping snooter buried in the matted fur. It didn't help that it had lain in the mud for some time, so I dragged not only the pelt but also what felt like half a ton of mud along the street.

The effort would be worth it to see the joy on Zandra's face when I dropped this delight on her bed. But I needed to hurry. We had somewhere wonderful to be this evening, and although this was a rare find, I wasn't missing the reopening of Gingerbread Bakery. I'd been dreaming about the sausage and bacon triple stack baps for weeks.

I kept out of sight from the neighbors as I got closer to home. I didn't want anyone attempting to steal this prize from me, not after it took me an hour to dig it out of the ground and drag it all this way. My glorious white fur was filthy, but a quick bath in the sink with Zandra's special bath oils would see me shining again. As much as I pretended I detested baths, I'd grown fond of them since joining with my witch.

No! I mustn't think like that. I must be as cat-like as possible. With the loss of my tail and several more clumps of fur falling out over the last month, I was worried I was turning into a mutant creature no one would recognize. And no one would want. A cat did not enjoy bathing in luxurious oils. No matter how delicious they smelled.

Still, my witch didn't judge based on appearance. But I missed being as magnificent as I used to be on the outside. Of course, I was glorious within, but sometimes people didn't take the time to explore that side of me.

I grunted as I pulled the heavy pelt up the wooden porch steps, and after a moment, I managed to open the front door and dragged my prize into the hallway. The place was quiet, since Vorana Stowell and Sage had gone to assist Tia and Binky with the bakery reopening. I left only a small trail of dirt on the wooden floorboards as I backed along, pulling the pelt with me.

I heard Zandra in our basement apartment, bumping things around. I'd timed it just right. She'd have a few minutes to admire the pelt then help me get clean, and then we'd be off to feast on the glorious free food Tia would provide as part of the celebration now her bakery was finally open again.

"Juno! Are you up there?" Zandra called out, her voice muffled.

I dropped the pelt and shook dirt off me, scattering it across Vorana's favorite rug. "Close your eyes. I have a surprise for you."

"Hurry. We're going to be late. There's already a big crowd there, according to Vorana. There might not be any sausage and bacon baps left if we don't get a wriggle on."

"Are your eyes closed?"

"What are you up to?" Zandra's voice carried a cynical note.

"It's a surprise. Don't spoil it."

"Is that what you've been doing? Organizing a surprise for me?"

"Yes! I'm coming down. Turn your back and cover your eyes. I don't want you peeking and spoiling the fun."

"Fine. Just get down here."

I left the pelt and hurried halfway down the steps, giving a nod when I saw Zandra couldn't see me. Then I dashed back up the stairs and bumped the pelt down them.

"What are you doing?" Zandra asked.

"Don't look! I need to get it ready before you see." I dropped the pelt and spent a few seconds smoothing it out, failing to dislodge the large chunks of dried-on mud. But Zandra would see beyond the dirt to the true beauty I'd discovered for her.

"Something stinks. Juno, have you stepped in something you shouldn't?"

"Of course not." I inspected my grubby front paws. "Well, maybe."

"You'd better not fight me if I decide you need a bath."

"I was thinking exactly the same thing."

She sighed. "Can I turn around?"

"Open your eyes." I danced on my paws, excited to see her reaction to such a wonderful gift.

Zandra turned and lowered her hands. She stared at me. "You're filthy! What have you been doing?"

"Don't mind me. What do you think?" I gestured my head at the squirrel pelt I'd lovingly laid out. "Half of its tail is still attached. It must have been a big male when it was alive. A real bruiser."

Zandra's jaw dropped open, and her pale skin lost any hint of color. "Is that... a squirrel?"

"Yes! I think there's still some flesh left on the tail."

She gagged. "It's the most revolting thing I've ever seen. Why did you drag it back here?"

"For you! I've always promised you that one day I'd present you with a squirrel. And here it is. Aren't I the perfect familiar?"

"It's rotting! And you've left bits of it all down the stairs. Vorana will freak if you've made a mess of her hallway."

"Give it a quick brush-down and you can hang it on the wall."

"You expect me to hang a decaying squirrel on our wall?"

"People put stuffed heads of wild animals they've shot on walls. Why not one of my kills?"

She arched an eyebrow. "Did you actually kill this thing?"

"Not exactly. But I found it. That means it belongs to me."

Zandra wrinkled her nose and crouched as she inspected the pelt. "How long has it been dead?"

"Not long. A few weeks. It still smells. That's how I found it."

"And you dug it up? Is that how you got in such a mess?"

"If we hurry, you could wash it, dry it in Vorana's tumble dryer, and then fashion it into a scarf. Everyone at the bakery opening will be so impressed."

Zandra turned ash gray. "I'm not wrapping a dead piece of animal around my throat. And it's not going on the wall either. You have to stop doing this."

"But I'm a cat familiar. It's what I do. You adore my gifts."

She tipped back her head and sighed. "Sure, you're a cat, but you're so much more than that. Your magic is like nothing I've ever felt before. And, you're—"

"I'm beautiful, unique, and the best familiar you'll ever have?"

Zandra grinned. "All of those things. But you don't have to keep playing up your cat side to me. I've had ten mice, fifteen shrews, and part of a rat's head on the bed in the last few weeks. It's too much. And you've started meowing."

I hissed to myself. I'd gone too far with trying to be the perfect feline companion. "I... I thought you'd like it. It's what other cats do."

"Not magical familiars."

I cocked my head. "Ember used to do it for Vorana."

"To make her feel sorry for him and to manipulate her. Don't do that to me," she said. "And you must find a new hobby. One that doesn't involve killing things and bringing them here. I'll never get some of those stains out of the bed sheets."

I glared at the squirrel pelt. This was all its fault. It wasn't good enough for my witch.

"Don't get sulky." Zandra stood and lifted me into her arms but held me out. "No snuggles for you. Not until you've had that bath. This'll make us so late." She carried me into the bathroom and filled the sink with warm water.

My head was down. "I had to bring you that pelt. I thought it would make you happy."

"I'd have been happier if you showed up on time. If you hadn't found that gross thing, we'd be at the bakery by now, stuffing our faces. I can't wait to try Tia's new pasties."

I submitted to being rubbed down with Zandra's cedarwood-scented soap and even let her massage each paw until the dirt was gone. "They sound delicious. Tia is thrilled with the sponsorship deal with Mystical Morsels."

"The last time we saw her, she was practically bouncing off the walls with excitement," Zandra said. "She was even talking about opening new bakeries, maybe setting up a franchise if it goes well."

"I'm happy for her, but I'm most excited about the free food Mystical Morsels is providing."

"Which is why we need to be there now. Everyone in town planned on dropping by and grabbing food. And I heard from Sorcha there'll be press coverage too. A camera crew! That's always popular with the locals. Everyone wants their five seconds of fame." Zandra vigorously rubbed my fur, her face scrunching into a frown.

My witch wasn't a fan of the media. She preferred to keep to the shadows and get things done. I was more accustomed to being recognized, but I stuck with Zandra and respected her wishes to avoid the limelight.

"How did Tia organize press coverage?" I asked.

"She didn't. It's part of the sponsorship deal, apparently. Gingerbread Bakery is about to go global!"

"Maybe we should get on camera." I shuffled back so she could properly massage my belly. "It's important the world knows how amazing you are. And it would be fun to get interviewed. You could send a copy of the recording to Tempest and the others, showing us stuffing our faces."

Zandra laughed. "It would put Wiggles' nose out of joint to see you as the star."

"He already knows that's the truth, but it never hurts to remind him."

Zandra lifted me out of the sink and gave me a thorough towel drying. It was my most favorite part of being bathed. She returned to the sink and stared at it. "You're still losing fur. I should take you to the vet. You didn't use to shed like this."

I hissed softly. "No vets. They only make things worse. It must be my hormones."

"Hormones? If you say so. But let me know if you're not feeling good. There's no point hiding it until you get too sick."

"I'm fine. I'm just going through a few changes." I focused on licking what was left of my fur back into shape, forcing myself not to focus on losing my tail and now my gorgeous fur.

Ten minutes later, after Zandra had cleaned up the mud and decayed bits of squirrel I'd trailed through the house, we dashed into town to celebrate the opening of Gingerbread Bakery with everyone else.

As we got closer to the bakery, we spotted a mass of people standing around. Everyone was eating, and the air was filled with a tantalizing medley of aromas. The scent of sizzling meat and the irresistible fragrance of freshly baked bread enticed my taste buds. And amidst the delicious scents, the sounds of laughter, chatter, and clinking utensils filled the air.

I drooled as I contemplated the mountain of food that awaited me.

The ground shook as Binky ran over to me. She was Tia's magnificent cougar familiar and had startling amber eyes and a glossy coat. She greeted me with a head-butt and nodded at Zandra.

"Everyone's here! I don't know whether I should be nervous or excited that the bakery has gathered such a huge crowd."

"It looks amazing," Zandra said. "All the hard work to get it open has been worth it."

I nodded. The building had been covered with plastic, and the windows blocked out with soap so no one could see the renovations following a recent magical explosion, but now it was open for everyone to explore.

I squeezed through the crowd with Zandra and Binky and peered inside the bakery. Soft, golden lighting accentuated the charm of the wooden interior. Freshly baked croissants, cinnamon rolls, and delicate pastries filled the new glass display counter, neatly arranged and tempting the eyes. Shelves lined with artisan bread and delectable cakes showcased Tia's magnificent baking skills. And alongside the new sign for the Gingerbread Bakery was the logo of Mystical Morsels, a sparkling pasty with a halo.

"Hey! They have free samples." Zandra stared at the four long tables set next to the bakery and rubbed her hands together.

"When can we get inside? I see sausage and bacon baps." My stomach growled.

Binky gave a throaty laugh. "Soon. Tia's talking to Celeste Hearthstone. She's the big shot from Mystical Morsels. They want to get pictures of the crowd and do interviews. But once the doors are open, it'll be a free-for-all, so get ready. And Mystical Morsels is footing the bill, so you can eat your fill once you're inside."

"I'm getting samples before that. You in?" Zandra said to me.

"Try and stop me." I trotted to the samples tables and investigated the food. There were cubes of different breads, bagels, buns, rolls, and biscuits, alongside a variety of cured meats. Cookies, mini cakes and fruit pies, muffin chunks, snack cakes, and a range of sweet rolls had all been cut into bite-sized morsels.

Binky came with me and sniffed the offerings. "How's Sammy doing?"

"Good. He'll be back soon. He's still having daily rehab with Tinkerbell. It's helping. His magic seems more stable, but there's still a way to go before Angel Force considers him safe." I tried a thin slice of roasted meat and added it to the paper sample pot I'd picked up.

"I'll have to visit soon. I tried once, but Barney said Sammy wasn't allowed visitors yet."

"Only one or two. His magic is still unpredictable." Ever since Tinkerbell and Sammy got arrested for their involvement in almost destroying Crimson Cove and letting it be taken over by gremlins, they'd been undergoing intensive magical rehab to get back on their paws. Sammy was responding better than Tinkerbell, who was her usual grumpy, stubborn-headed self, but Sammy had the added complication of a werewolf potion running through his system, so his recovery was slower than I'd like.

I filled the pot with delicious samples, from dried salami to tiny chunks of caramel cake with a frosted cream topping. I was about to leave the table when Finn dashed past, almost treading on Binky's tail.

"Hey! What's the hurry?" I asked.

Finn turned and looked down at me. For a second, he didn't seem to recognize me, but then he blinked, and his usual charming smile appeared on his handsome angel face. "Juno! Sorry, lost in my thoughts. Enjoying the party?"

I tilted my head. "All is well here. But not with you. What's the matter?"

He looked around and tugged at his crumpled white shirt. "Ever get the feeling you're being watched?"

"Only when I'm actually being watched. It's a predator-prey thing. Why? Is someone stalking you?" I glanced around the crowd, but no one paid Finn any special attention. They were too busy eating and gossiping, as should be the case at all good parties.

"Finn! There you are. I've been looking for you." A short, round-faced woman of around fifty with a severe, cropped dark bob marched over. She barely came up to Finn's chest but radiated righteous indignation that made my ears twitch. "Augustus and Dawn are here."

Finn nodded. "That's fine. I said they could come to the opening. They've been looking forward to it."

The woman's stern expression darkened. "I told them they had to stay at the sanctuary."

He let out a gentle sigh. "That wasn't necessary."

"Greetings!" I said to her. "We've not met."

Finn ran a hand through his sandy brown hair. "Juno, this is Hortense Scornbloom. She's been volunteering at the animal sanctuary for the last two months."

I nodded a friendly hello, which she ignored.

"They're drinking whiskey!" Hortense jammed her hands on her hips. "That's unprofessional. And they won't listen to me when I tell them to behave."

Finn rested a hand on her shoulder. "Hortense, you're all volunteers. And I can't force them to stay at the sanctuary if they don't want to be there. They said they'd stop by for half an hour and then go back. The animals will be fine. We don't have any special cases that need around-the-clock care. Everything is under control."

She shrugged off his hand. "There are jobs to complete. I told them what they needed to do, but they ignored me."

"That's because you're not our boss." A young woman with straight red hair and a huge half-eaten pasty in one hand marched over. A tall, thin man with a beard down to his waist accompanied her.

"Don't talk back to me, young lady. Respect your elders," Hortense said.

The young woman matched Hortense scowl for scowl. "How can I respect you when you're always on my case, trying to cause trouble for me?"

"Dawn, let's all get along," Finn said. "This is a party. You know, eating, drinking, music, laughter. More eating. How's the pasty?"

"It's not Dawn's fault they're fighting," the bearded man said. "Hortense is being bitchy. She's worse than me."

Finn groaned. "Not you, too, Augustus?"

"I'm only scolding them because they're not listening to sense," Hortense said.

"You don't have the right to boss us around." Dawn shoved a large chunk of pasty in her mouth and chewed furiously.

"Excuse me, may I take a few shots of you in action?" A guy wearing a red bandana and sporting a sizeable pot belly held a camera on his shoulder as he stood in front of us. "I'm capturing vibes for an opening montage. You good with that?"

Hortense shoved past him, almost knocking the camera off his shoulder. "I already said no. Leave me out of this and don't publish any footage of me because you don't have my permission. I shouldn't have wasted my time coming here. People are idiots. I'm going back to the sanctuary."

"Hortense! Don't be like that," Finn called after her. "Go grab a plate of food and let your hair down."

"Let her go. She's a nightmare." Augustus flicked his beard over one shoulder. "She doesn't know how to enjoy herself. Hortense is only happy when she's bossing us around."

"You mean she's rude! I can't stand her," Dawn said. "She thinks she owns the place, but she's no better than us."

Finn puffed out a breath. "Hortense works hard."

"She works hard at making our lives miserable." Dawn ate more pasty, dropping crumbs on the ground. She waved at the guy with the camera. "You can interview us if you like."

He stared at her crumb-strewn clothing and walked away.

"I'll talk to her again. See if I can get her to dial things down," Finn said. "I know you can all get along. You share a love of animals, so you have that in common. Isn't that enough?"

Dawn and Augustus both shrugged and walked off into the crowd, their heads bent together.

"Are the new recruits causing you trouble?" I asked.

"You don't know the half of it. Hortense thinks she's in charge, and it's causing tension. She's good at what she does, but I don't know if it's worth the hassle to keep her on. Even the animals get nervous around her when she raises her voice." Finn jumped and looked around. "I could swear someone is watching me. I keep getting shivers up and down my spine."

I looked around the crowd again, but everyone was enjoying themselves and still paying Finn no attention. "Go get some food and relax. Keep an eye on Zandra for me, though. She's over with Vorana and Sage."

"Will do. What you gonna do?"

I inspected my full pot of food. "I have somewhere I need to be."

Chapter 2

Magical interlude

I hurried away from the excited, food munching crowd and over to the animal control office. Sammy and Tinkerbell would be back soon from their rehab session, and I wanted to be there to see how Sammy was doing.

As I walked along the main corridor, Glenda Ridgeback was coming out of the holding room, where injured or misbehaving magical critters were kept. She smirked when she saw me. "I don't need to guess why you're here."

"Are they back?" I'd been returning to animal control most evenings after work to spend time with Sammy. He wasn't always up to seeing me, but I still sat on the other side of the door and talked to him about my day and ideas I had for things he could do when his rehab finished.

"They're back. But I should warn you, Tinkerbell's being sassy. She tried to bite me."

"She's a bad influence on Sammy." My hackles lifted. "She shouldn't be here."

"Tinkerbell's got an attitude as twisted as a black magic using witch who's about to be burned at the stake, but she is making improvements most days. Sadly, this isn't one of those days. What have you got in there?" Glenda gestured at the pot.

"Treats for Sammy, so hands off." Werewolves were notoriously greedy, and a fine specimen like Glenda needed enormous meals to keep those curves in tip-top shape.

Glenda chuckled and lifted a hand. "No worries. I've got snacks in the kitchen. See you tomorrow." She wandered along the corridor and disappeared out of sight.

I nosed the door open and walked to Sammy's regular pen, which was housed next to Tinkerbell. To my astonishment, there was an unexpected arrival in the room. "Ember Dreamscape!"

He sat two cages over from Sammy. "Juno. It's good to see you."

"I can't say the same. What are you doing here?" Ember had grown since I'd encountered him as a gangly kitten. His black and white fur gleamed, and his eyes were bright. He was a handsome young cat.

"He's a turncoat," Tinkerbell said.

"He's not. Ember's doing the right thing at last," Sammy said. "Hi, Juno. Your fur looks nice."

"What's left of it," Tinkerbell muttered.

"You smell good, too."

"Thank you. I've had a bath." Sammy's dull tabby fur didn't smell too sweet. The toxic magic swirling through him seeped out of his paws, making him smell like a damp badger who'd rolled in fox droppings. I focused on Ember. "The last I heard about you, you were about to go behind bars for twenty years."

Ember dropped his head. "I've changed. I'm being a better cat."

"Like I said, he snitched," Tinkerbell said. "He turned on the gremlins and has agreed to testify against them. So much for them being his only family."

My eyes widened. "You have?"

Ember sank on to his belly. "I know now what Gaian and Lila did was wrong. But at the time, they were all I knew, and I'd been with them since I was a kitten. They saved my life after I got dumped, so I didn't want to turn my back on them."

"You were quick enough to ditch them when you were promised no time inside," Tinkerbell said. "Traitor."

"You're traitors too," Ember said. "When the time comes, we're all testifying against them. It's not my fault you were too dumb to see they were using you and Sammy. At least they loved me. They thought you were pathetic and dumped you the second your usefulness ran out."

Tinkerbell spat at him and slashed a murder mitten through the air. "If there weren't bars separating us, you'd be flat on your back, begging for your pointless life."

"Glad to see your rehab is working so well." I smiled at Sammy and nudged the pot of treats closer.

"Rehab is a waste of time," Tinkerbell retorted. "Some creatures can't be changed. Nor should they."

"Everyone can change if they want to," I said. "Whether you think you can or you think you can't achieve something, you'll prove yourself right."

"Don't waste your psychobabble on me." Tinkerbell lifted her nose and sniffed. "Is some of that food for me?"

"That's for Sammy to decide," I said. "Maybe you should be nicer, though, or you won't deserve treats."

"Suck it. I don't want your lousy treats, anyway." She turned her back on me and flicked her tail.

I eyeballed Ember but then focused on my beloved Sammy. He looked better than a month ago. He was eating regularly and no longer appeared so defeated, but there was still some way to go, and I could feel the sticky unpleasantness of his contaminated magic lingering in the air every time I got close.

Sammy flicked me a glance then looked away, sensing I was examining him.

"You should be happy Juno is here," Ember said.

"Of course I'm happy," Sammy said. "But she's way too good for me. I don't know why you bother."

"I bother because we have a history, most of it good. And your illness wasn't your fault."

"You still feel responsible for that, don't you?" Sammy pulled a small piece of dried meat out of the pot with his paw and ate it.

"He's always talking about you," Ember said.

"When have you been gossiping about me?" I flashed Ember a warning snarl. I'd been on the wrong end of this young cat's deceit before, so wouldn't be so easily tricked again.

"We often meet at rehab. We go to the same place. I think he loves you."

"And how would you know that, since you're supposed to be behind bars being punished and not sharing secrets with Sammy?" I snapped at Ember. I hadn't forgiven him for his treachery, nor the way he'd mistreated Sage and Vorana to get what he wanted.

"Don't be mean to him," Sammy said. "They found something weird going on with Ember's magic, so they've been giving him special treatment. He's been having it daily for two weeks."

I stared at Sammy in surprise. "You never said."

"I knew you'd worry if I told you we were back in contact."

He was right to think that. The young cat couldn't be trusted.

"It's working," Ember said. "With this treatment and now that I'm testifying against the gremlins, I'm hopeful I can get out soon. Then I can find someone to bond with."

"No one will want you," Tinkerbell said. "You're damaged goods. The star of the academy, taken in by a pair of deceitful gremlins. No magic user will ever trust you. Not if they have more than a few brain cells."

I zapped Tinkerbell in the butt with a stinging spell. "You're talking about yourself."

"Like I want to get saddled with a pathetic magic user who carries me around like some oversized baby and feeds me until I'm so fat I can barely walk." She glanced over her shoulder at me.

My fur bristled. I was soft around the middle, but who could resist the delicious treats Vorana served?

The door opened, and Barney Hoffman, head of animal control, stepped in. "Oh! I didn't realize we had visitors. Evening, Juno. I've come to see Ember... and everyone else."

"I didn't realize Ember was coming back to Crimson Cove," I said. "Some warning would have been nice."

Barney's cheeks flushed. "Sorry. It was a last-minute thing. I've been in negotiation with Angel Force over Ember's treatment and sentencing, and they finally made a decision about what to do with him. It shouldn't have taken so long, but you know how slowly the angels can move."

"Half a dozen committee meetings, a thirty-page document of the pros and cons, and then the outcome needing to be signed off by the higher angels?"

He chuckled and scrubbed a hand across his whiskered cheeks. "Something like that. Ember, perhaps we could go for a walk? Leave Juno and Sammy to talk."

Ember hopped onto his paws and chirruped. "I'd like that. I've been looking forward to it ever since you suggested it."

"Ember's not safe to take out of that pen!" I said.

"Juno, I promise you, I'm getting better. And Barney believes in me," Ember insisted.

I glowered at Barney, checking to see if his pupils were dilated. "Are you under this cat's influence? You can't believe a word he says."

"No! Nothing like that. But I want to help Ember. He's young and impressionable, and he wants to turn over a new leaf, but he needs a guiding hand. Don't worry, I'll have restraints on him at all times, and it'll only be a short walk around the block."

"We could go to the park," Ember said. "I'd love to feel the grass under my paws. Much better than these pens."

"Let's take this slowly." Barney lifted glowing magical restraints from his pocket. "I'm trusting you not to misbehave."

Ember lifted his tail. "I'm happy to get out of here. Leave the two lovebirds to it."

I was less than thrilled Barney was taking such a risk. Although Ember sounded like he'd changed, my trust in him was lost, so I expected the worst from him.

"We won't be long. Oh, Juno, your visitor left a message. She'll be here in a few minutes. She didn't sound happy, though," Barney said. "She growled at me."

"Thanks, Barney. I'll meet her at the door when she arrives."

I kept a sharp eye on Ember as he left. He chirped away happily and chatted to Barney and seemed genuinely thrilled to be with him. I'd keep an eye on that tricksy creature to make sure he didn't have another con under way.

"I don't trust him," I murmured to Sammy.

"He's much better," Sammy said around a mouthful of meat. "He's changed for the better."

"You're an idiot if you believe that," Tinkerbell said. "Toss me some of that food. I'm starving."

I looked at her, gesturing towards her kibble bowl, and shook my head. Tinkerbell was only ever happy when she was complaining.

"Who's your visitor?" Sammy asked.

"Grace Laker. I contacted her again and pressed upon her the importance of your recovery."

"You've been ordering a werewolf about?" Tinkerbell sniggered. "I look forward to attending your funeral. That's if I'm out in time."

"You won't get an invitation."

"Be careful around the werewolves," Sammy cautioned. "They don't play nicely with outsiders."

"They know better than to tangle with me. Especially when their lies led to your illness. I'll be back in a moment. Keep eating." I left the room and hurried to the main door. Just as I got there, there was a rapid knock.

I opened it to find Grace outside, dressed in a smart soft gray pant suit. She'd been married to Emron Laker, a deceased jerk of a werewolf, and came from an ancient and powerful line of werewolves. Her family founded the Golden Pentacle pack, but Grace now lived a reclusive life in Pentacle Ridge. We'd become acquainted when investigating her husband's demise.

She nodded at me, her expression cold. "I got what you need."

"Perfect. Come in," I said.

Grace shook her head and placed a small glass vial in front of me. "I can't stay. But I did the digging as you demanded. This is the best I can provide as an antidote."

I inspected the glowing purple liquid. "Will this get me my Sammy back?"

A flicker of regret crossed her sharply beautiful face. "Maybe. Partially. He'll never be quite the same, though."

"Sammy will be better? He won't be troubled by dark thoughts and the desire to use illegal magic once he's taken this antidote?"

She sighed. "There are no guarantees. The werewolf potion that hit him was ancient and the magic warped. There could be a few side effects after he takes this."

"What kind of side effects?" I sniffed the bottle, but the cork masked the scent.

"They'll be temporary, most likely. He'll be extra tired to begin with, though. I went to the best werewolf potion mixer we've got. If this doesn't help, nothing will."

"So long as it doesn't make him any sicker," I said.

Her face tightened. "Tread carefully, Juno. I spent time, effort, and a considerable amount of money getting that for you. It'll work. Now, are we done?"

I nodded. "We're done."

"Good. I only helped because of the mess my dumb husband caused. No more favors, got it?"

"Understood."

Grace nodded and strode away to a large, dark SUV. She slid inside. I picked up the potion in my mouth and dashed back to the room.

"What have you got there?" Sammy asked.

I set down the potion and explained what I'd done. An expression of hopeful cautiousness crossed his face. "You still care for me?"

My toe beans tingled. "Of course I do."

"Then you're dumber than you look," Tinkerbell said. "You've wasted money and effort on some quackery werewolf placebo. Sammy will start howling at the moon if he drinks that."

I ignored her. "The werewolves had to help since they caused this problem. Grace said it may not be perfect, but it'll help you stop desiring dark magic."

Sammy squeezed his eyes shut for a second. "I want that. I want to feel normal again. I don't want to have these cravings for something I know is so bad for me."

"Let's hope it stops him from craving so much food," Tinkerbell said. "I know you sneak kibble from my bowl when I'm asleep."

Sammy huffed out a breath. "I do not! And even if I did, it's a side effect of the rehab drugs. They make me extra hungry."

I pulled the treat pot away from him, pulled out the cork, and poured the contents of the vial into the remaining treats. A woody, menthol scent filled the room.

"What do you think of the food?" I asked.

Sammy nodded, his attention on the pot. "It's good."

"It won't taste good now that stuff's been mixed into it," Tinkerbell sniped.

"It's from Gingerbread Bakery. Tia's reopening today," I said.

"I'd have loved to have been there," Sammy said. "I miss the bakery. Tia makes the most amazing food."

"It's bigger and better," I said. "Tia's done a deal with Mystical Morsels. There was a huge crowd there, and she's getting press coverage." I kept mixing, hoping my chat about the bakery would distract Sammy from his worries and lessen his nerves before he downed a potion that may not help him.

"I miss everyone," Sammy said softly. "I miss Archie, Binky, even Elijah. Did I tell you, he stopped by to see me the other evening?"

"I didn't know that," I said.

"He told me I looked terrible and out of shape."

"Typical Elijah." I did a final swirl of the potion and left it to settle for a minute. "When you're fully back on your paws, I could take you to the bakery for a supervised visit. My treat."

"I'd love that. Maybe... maybe it could be a date? You know, like old times?"

"Never gonna happen," Tinkerbell chimed in.

"You be quiet," I snapped at her.

"I tell it like it is."

I made a point of turning my back on her, just like she'd done to me. "Let's take this one step at a time. You've got a lot of healing to do."

Sammy sighed. "I get it. You've moved on. There must be dozens of eligible familiars around here interested in you."

"Not looking like that, they won't be," Tinkerbell muttered.

"I'm too busy with work and my wonderful witch to think about anything like that," I said.

"You're not seeing anyone?" Sammy asked.

I pushed the pot back toward him. "Eat up. Let's see what this does for you."

Sammy lowered his head then nodded and scooped out the contents of the pot, eating it in two big bites.

"How do you feel?" I watched him closely for any reaction.

"Sleepy." He fell onto his side, twitched a couple of times, then began snoring.

"Looks like you killed him," Tinkerbell said.

"I'll kill someone in here if she doesn't keep her mouth shut," I muttered.

The door opened again, and Sorcha Creer poked her head inside. "Hey, Juno. How's Sammy doing?"

"He's fine. Or he will be. Don't make too much noise, though. He's sleeping." I did a final check on Sammy then headed over to Sorcha. "Good luck if you're here to see Tinkerbell. She's got her extra mean, evil face on tonight, and she's taking no prisoners."

Sorcha rolled her eyes. "Some things never change. I'll soon get her purring."

"Watch over Sammy while you're here," I said. "I just gave him something. It should help, but he passed out the second he took it."

"Of course. Whatever you need. Zandra was asking where you were," Sorcha said. "She found some salmon mousse she thought you'd enjoy."

"I'm on my way back now." Salmon mousse sounded like the perfect palate cleanser after Tinkerbell's sharpness.

"I won't stay long, so I'll catch up with you later," Sorcha said. "Tia's got a huge celebration cake, so I don't want to miss out on a slice."

"Sure. Pick food over me," Tinkerbell groused.

Leaving Sorcha with the spiky Tinkerbell and the snoozing Sammy, I walked along the corridor. I hoped the werewolf potion would help Sammy. His rehabilitation was painfully slow, and Angel Force was threatening to put him away if he didn't turn a corner soon. But I refused to write him off. Sammy would get better.

The door along the corridor opened, and Randal Nix bounded out, an empty coffee mug in one hand. He pushed his glasses up his nose, and his cheeks flushed bright red. "Hey... Um... I've been waiting for you to finish with Sammy. May I have a word?"

"Always. I find the word 'maleficent' or 'serendipity' have a nice mouth feel. What do you think?"

His laugh sounded awkward. "Yeah, they're great words. I... I need your advice."

"I'm always willing to give advice. About what?"

"It's about Zandra." Randal inspected the empty mug. "How do you think she'd react if I asked her out again?"

Chapter 3

Double date?

A huge, catlike smile crossed my face. "I've already approved of you dating Zandra."

"Thanks. But it's not so much your approval I'm seeking." Randal gripped his coffee mug so tightly I became concerned it might shatter. "I don't know if she still likes me. Or even if she ever did. And the last time we dated, it ended badly."

"It didn't even begin! Your meal was abandoned because of an emergency. Zandra always does the right thing, even if that means leaving you before the main course is underway. I'm sure you admire that fine quality in my wonderful witch."

"I know. And I do! She's awesome. But... maybe it's a sign," Randal said.

I tilted my head. "A sign you need to try again?"

"A sign I should learn my lesson and not ask Zandra out again. But I can't stop thinking about her. I'm always professional when we work together, but she's great. I really like her. A lot."

"Of course you have an ocean of like for Zandra. My witch is most pleasing," I said. "Anyone who dates her should feel privileged they even breathe the same air."

He chuckled. "Yeah, that's what I meant. I want to try again, but maybe I should go about it differently."

"Ask Zandra out again, but keep things simple. Maybe not a meal this time. You could start with a coffee and a walk. Something to keep you both occupied and less nervous."

Randal grimaced. "I get so nervous around her. No, this was a mistake. I'm the one with the issue. I need to understand she's way out of my league and move on."

I lifted my front paws and rested them on Randal's calf. "No one will ever be in Zandra's league, but she still deserves to date and be happy. And you could make her happy. This is perfect! Love is in the air, with Cythera and her fiancé planning their wedding, and you and Zandra dating again. You could double date. I'll chaperone."

"That sounds terrifying," Randal said. "Zandra and Cythera would kill each other by the end of the night."

"I doubt they'd go that far, but it would be entertaining." I chuckled to myself as I imagined the couples going on a double date together. Randal and Maverick would behave, but my witch and Cythera could end up pulling each other's hair out.

Randal scratched his fingers through his already messy hair. "I don't know how to ask Zandra, though. I figured you'd have some ideas. Something that would make her say yes."

"Are you busy now?" I asked.

"I'm always busy, but it's nothing urgent."

I paused. "And you are sticking around? You were only supposed to be in Crimson Cove while you completed the upgrade. That upgrade came and went some time ago."

A smile crossed his face. "You're worried I might skip town after capturing Zandra's heart?"

"If you were fortunate enough to capture her heart, you'd never leave her side. But I don't want her getting invested in something fleeting. Or someone who has no plan to remain close by."

"I'd never do that. Well, I may have to go away for a few weeks. I cover a lot of ground with this job, but I've arranged it so I can work wherever I like, and I've decided to stay in Crimson Cove for a while. Maybe forever if things work out."

That was what I wanted to hear. "Let's go." I turned and headed along the corridor toward the exit.

Randal hurried behind me. "Wait! Where are we going?"

"To start your date with Zandra. No time like the present."

"I'm not ready. I haven't gone through my date questions. And I haven't changed my T-shirt in days."

"You smell fine. And you don't need a list of questions for a date. When you're not panicking about what to say to Zandra, you get along fine. Treat this date like another day at the office, without the rules."

"The rules? I'm confused. What rules should I follow? Or what rules shouldn't I follow?" Randal stumbled after me. "Juno! Help! I'm not prepared. I can't mess this up."

I stopped by the door and turned to him. "Put down that mug, tidy your hair, and take a breath before you pass out."

"What if I mess this up and jeopardize Zandra's friendship?"

"She's an ideal friend, as long as you don't get on her prickly side. But you want more. And I have a feeling she does, too." I gave him a once-over. Randal was his typically messy, geekily handsome self, but since Zandra liked that look, I made no suggestions on physical improvements. "Let's move."

He spluttered a few more protests as we left animal control and headed to Gingerbread Bakery, but I brushed them away. My witch deserved a nice guy, and I hadn't met a nicer guy than Randal Nix in a long time.

We slowed as the street grew crowded.

"I don't see Zandra. Are you sure she's here?" Randal stood on his tiptoes as he looked around.

"She's over there, helping Tia and Finn load that van. Keep up." I trotted along, with Randal lagging behind. "Don't lose your determination now. Just think, in a few minutes, you'll be having a date, and Zandra won't even be aware of it."

"I hope this is the right thing to do," he muttered.

"It is. But if it falls apart and Zandra decides she can't stand the sight of you, I'll be happy to chase you out of town."

"Thanks, Juno."

"Stop getting in our way. Can't you see we're busy?" Hortense was shooing away the camera crew. Standing with them was a well-dressed woman in a tailored green dress that swept the ground. She had silver bangles on her wrists and long dark hair. Her appearance was striking. I'd even go as far as to say she was beautiful.

"Need a helping paw?" I stopped by the van that was being loaded with food.

Tia turned to me. "Thanks, but we're almost done. Hi, Randal. Nice to see you here. Couldn't stay away from the free food, huh?"

"Something like that." Randal was looking at Zandra, who was piling up a stack of boxes. "Juno thought it was a good idea for me to get out of the office. Um... If you'll excuse me, I need to speak to Zandra."

A knowing smile crossed Tia's face. "Of course. See you later. He's still hung up on her, isn't he?" she said the second Randal was out of earshot.

"Naturally. Who wouldn't be? What's going on?"

Tia pointed to the camera crew Hortense was telling off. "You see that woman over there? The one with the pretty dress?"

"I was just admiring it. Who is she?"

"Celeste Hearthstone. She's the chief executive of Mystical Morsels. I didn't expect her to come to the opening, but she said she wouldn't miss it. She arranged all the media for the event and even paid for the food. But then she surprised me by showing up with more food to donate to local charities. Of course, Finn stepped in and said his sanctuary would welcome all donations. So we're loading it up, and he's going back there with his volunteers. Some of it can be stored, but the rest will be eaten or given to the animals. Celeste's something else. So generous."

I studied the attractive woman as she talked quietly to Hortense. I couldn't hear their conversation, but whatever she was saying to Hortense, it didn't make her happy.

"What's Hortense's problem?" I asked. "She was snippy with the other volunteers earlier this evening."

Tia scowled into the crowd. "Don't ask me. She always has to pick a fight with someone. I wish she wasn't here. She's been making a nuisance of herself."

"Hortense doesn't seem to like Celeste. How do they know each other?"

"I don't think they do. Hortense likes no one," Tia said.

The sharpness in her voice surprised me. "She's been causing you trouble, too?"

"Hortense is one of those people who's only content when she's making life hard for others." Tia nodded at Zandra as she loaded up the final boxes. "Is that the last of it?"

She nodded back. "All done."

"Did you see that Randal's here?" I said to Zandra. "He finished work early so he could enjoy your company."

Zandra grinned. "Yeah, I saw him. He's gone off to get us coffee. I wonder who twisted his arm to get him away from his gadgets?"

"I can't imagine, but they must be clever."

"They need to leave!" Hortense raised her voice as she gestured at the cameraman doing sweeping shots of the crowd.

I turned to see Finn had joined Hortense. "No, they don't. They're doing their jobs."

"They're poking around and asking questions. And the moron with the camera was rude to me!" Hortense swiped a hand through the air.

"You tried to take the camera off him. He had to defend himself."

"She damaged it. The woman's crazy." The camera guy stepped back as Hortense glared at him.

Finn guided her away from the camera crew and closer to us. "Go wait with the other volunteers. We'll be leaving soon."

She went red with anger, not happy at being told what to do, but stomped off and stood with Dawn and Augustus, who didn't greet her with warm hugs and smiles.

Finn walked over to us, his wings drooping behind him. "I've reached my limit. I'm not sure I can do this for much longer."

"What are you talking about?" Zandra said.

"My job at Angel Force and the animal sanctuary. I thought my animal rescue would be a small thing, but as soon as I set it up, it grew, and it keeps growing. And after the trouble we had with the gremlins causing chaos in town, the animals are twitchy and not behaving well. I've had several new, difficult critters arrive. They need treatment and weeks of rehab." He rubbed the back of his neck. "Too much more, and I'll break."

"You need an assistant," I said.

"I'd love one, but how will I pay for that? The sanctuary isn't a profit-making venture. I do it for the love, not the money. I figured having extra volunteers would help, but it's added another layer of issues." He gestured at the still scowling Hortense. "I was better off doing things on my own."

"Hortense seems tricky," Tia said. "Maybe she's not right for the sanctuary."

"She has her issues, but she always does her tasks to a high standard. I figured I could put up with her bossing people around, pretending she runs the place because she's so good at what she does, but I made a mistake." Finn rocked back on his heels. "There's so much we need to do at the sanctuary that I'll be there until midnight. And I've got the early shift tomorrow at Angel Force."

"Not if you have more help. Willing help, not grumpy volunteers. Zandra and Randal aren't doing anything tonight," I said.

"We aren't?" Randal showed up with two takeout mugs of coffee and handed one to Zandra.

I nodded. "They're willing to help at the sanctuary."

"I guess we can," Zandra said. "If that's okay with you, Randal?"

"Sure! I'd love to. I like it there. It could be a kind of date."

Zandra's eyes widened, and her cheeks grew pink. "I mean, could it? Won't we be mucking out stables and feeding animals?"

Randal gulped but pressed on. "A practical date. You know, no pressure. But only if you want to. I don't want to force you into it if you don't want to. Or... or we could do something else. After the animals. I mean, we need to help Finn. Or another day. Whatever you like. I... yeah. Whatever you want."

"Zandra wants to," I said. "We'll all go."

"What's this?" Celeste Hearthstone walked over with her camera crew behind her, smiling warmly at the group. "You're going to your animal rescue now, Finn?"

He nodded. "I figured we'd take the donations over there, and we always do final checks in the evenings to make sure everyone is settled in for the night."

"That sounds perfect. I'll join you. We can get some local ambiance on film and talk about the donations if that's okay with you?"

Finn shrugged, failing to hide his tiredness. "I have no problem with that. But it's not a tidy place. And the animals get boisterous when they see new faces."

"Even better! We adore supporting local causes." Celeste's warm smile widened. "How exciting. Shall we?"

Finn mustered a smile. "We shall."

After everyone had made arrangements to get to the sanctuary, we left town and made the short trip to the barns Finn rented to house his ever-growing menagerie of unwanted magical critters. The evening was drawing in, and a huge moon lit the road, giving a magical tinge to the evening. I made sure Randal rode in Zandra's van, and I allowed him to sit in my seat, so long as I was able to use his lap. He made for a comfortable perch.

"That looks like trouble." Zandra had stopped the van, and we sat watching as Hortense ordered Augustus and Dawn around, gesturing and pointing, her scowl severe.

"She loves to think she's in charge," I said.

We watched for another couple of minutes until Dawn and Augustus stomped off, leaving Hortense gesturing to herself.

"We'll stay out of her way," Zandra said. "Let's go see how we can help Finn."

Ten minutes later, we'd all been given tasks, and Zandra and Randal were put to work unloading the food from the van and sorting it into piles suitable for the animals.

I stood to one side, supervising, when an unpleasant sulfurous stink drifted up my booping snooter. It was accompanied by a waft of heat and the faint tang of the sea. My gaze settled on the dark shadows of the nearby trees. There was a brief flash of movement, but then it was gone.

I left my important supervising task and hurried over to Finn, who'd just finished an on-camera interview with Celeste.

"Do you need a job?" he asked.

"No, but I have a question. Have you got any dragons in rehab?"

He froze then blinked and laughed. "Why do you say that?"

"Because I smelled something dragon-like. If you're looking after an injured dragon, I need to know. Those things aren't to be trifled with."

His tongue traced across his bottom lip, and his gaze darted around. "Did you see a dragon or just get a whiff of one?"

"It was only a scent. Finn, I'm concerned. Is there a lethal killing machine in this animal sanctuary? If there is, my witch is vulnerable because we've not been told about it." I flexed my murder mittens. As much as I adored Finn, I wouldn't let him put Zandra in harm's way, especially if that harm was dragon-sized and spouted fire.

He crouched until we were almost eye level. "Juno, you've got nothing to worry about. There's no angry, injured dragon hiding in my barns."

"What's got you so nervous, then? And why am I smelling dragon?"

His head whipped around. "Do you still smell it?"

I stepped onto his booted foot to get his attention. "What aren't you telling me?"

He sighed, rolled his shoulders, and flexed his wings. "That I'm overworked, underpaid, and never get enough appreciation? I always put on the nice angel act, but I'm beat. It's too much for one guy to handle."

"We all appreciate you. But if you're hiding something—"

"No! Nothing. Sorry if I've been on edge recently. Work and this place are stressing me out, and I'm struggling to find a healthy balance. It's making me jittery. I'm not sleeping and drinking way too much caffeine."

"That's all?"

"Sure. Now, I need a hand with healing magic if you're up to the task. Some of the new intakes have injuries. Have you got any magic going spare?" Finn asked, his regular smile appearing.

I narrowed my eyes. Finn was usually an open book, but not this evening. I'd like to interrogate him further, but I hated the thought of injured animals being left untreated. "Show me where they are. I'll look after them."

He let out a sigh. "Great. You're the best, Juno. Follow me. They're in the isolation area."

Over the next two hours, I was kept busy, calming and healing half a dozen magical critters. Once they were sleeping comfortably and pain free, I left the isolation area and headed out to see how Zandra and Randal's date was going.

An ear-piercing shriek cut through the night and sent a shiver down my spine. I dashed toward the barn where the scream had come from.

Dawn was backing away from the door, her hands over her mouth. "She's dead!"

Chapter 4

Forked!

My heart was in my throat as I bounded toward the barn Dawn had shied away from. "Who's dead?"

Dawn lowered her hands, her face drained of color, and her body twitching in shock. "It's Hortense!"

The breath whooshed out of me. Of course, I didn't think for one second my witch had gotten herself in trouble, but I'd been so preoccupied helping the injured animals that I'd lost track of what she'd been doing. I hurried to the entrance of the barn. It was a simple storage area, mainly used for food and animal supplies, so there were no critters living inside. Hurried footsteps came from behind me as I made my way into the hay-scented area.

Hortense was on her back, a large hayfork sticking out of her chest. Her face was covered in crumbs.

I lifted my head and closed my eyes, feeling for any thread of her life force. The place was silent.

Not even a breeze swirling around me or a ghost breaking wind. It was too late to save her.

"Juno! What's going on?" Zandra was next inside the barn, followed by Randal.

"Oh! Did she fall?" Randal asked.

"She's on her back," I said. "I don't think this was an accident."

Finn rushed in. He hurried to Hortense and kneeled beside her. His fingers went to the pulse point on her neck, and he grimaced. "She's gone. Did anyone see what happened?"

"Your volunteer, Dawn, found her," I said. "It was her scream that alerted me something was wrong."

He looked around the barn. "Where is she?"

"The last time I saw her, she was outside," I said. "She appeared faint."

Finn stood and looked down at Hortense for a few seconds. "Everyone outside. There's nothing we can do here."

"Did someone do this to her?" Zandra asked him.

"It's possible, so we can't risk the evidence being contaminated. Everyone, get outside, and I'll close this up."

While Finn cajoled everyone out, which included several more volunteers and the camera crew, I hurried over and looked around the body. The cause of death seemed obvious, but there was a pungent, savory smell on the corpse, and Hortense was covered in crumbs, as if someone had crumbled a piece of bread over her after she'd fallen and scattered the crumbs over her face and shoulders.

Finn walked over and joined me. "You too, Juno. I don't want Cythera arriving and thinking you were involved."

"I wouldn't worry too much about that. She always thinks I'm guilty of something. Stealing her food. Teasing her angels. Murdering an innocent person. It's all the same to her." After another quick sniff, I went outside and joined Zandra, who stood with Tia.

"Hortense is really dead?" Tia asked. "It's such a shock. I didn't see her that long ago."

Zandra nodded. "She's gone. Looks like it only just happened, too."

"I didn't know you were joining us to volunteer," I said to Tia. "You must be exhausted after such a hectic day."

"I'm running on adrenaline fumes and caffeine, but I found more boxes of food in the bakery, so I figured I'd bring them over. We sold out of everything, so there was no point keeping the place open." Tia's wide eyes remained on the barn. "I don't think I'd been here ten minutes when I heard the scream. I can't believe it."

While Zandra and Tia talked about what had happened, I looked around the assembled group. Finn had disappeared, no doubt to contact Angel Force. The camera guy stood with Celeste. I couldn't tell if he was filming, but he had his camera on his shoulder, so he was most likely hoping to get a story out of this tragic event. Dawn and Augustus stood close together, muttering. Augustus was patting Dawn's shoulder while she talked, and they kept looking at the closed barn doors.

I inched closer, eager to hear what Dawn had to say. Since she'd discovered Hortense's body, she may have seen something useful. Maybe even the person who did it running away.

"Don't worry," Augustus said. "Everyone knew she had this coming. Mean old baggage."

Dawn sniffed. "I know it's about time someone shut her up for good, but I still feel bad. There was so much blood."

"Karma deals out revenge in the end," Augustus said. "And don't feel bad. Hortense was always mean to you."

"She was mean to everyone," Dawn said. "Finn told me I'd get used to it. I didn't, though."

"You stood up to her. It's more than I did. I just avoided her or smiled and nodded in the hope she'd go away."

"Greetings!" I said.

They both jumped.

"Who are you, beautiful?" Augustus asked. "You look familiar, but I'm certain you're not a resident at the sanctuary."

"No. I'm Juno, familiar to the most wonderful witch you'll ever have the privilege of meeting, Zandra Crypt. I couldn't help but overhear you talking about Hortense. I take it she wasn't popular?"

"What's it to you?" Dawn asked.

The trace of suspicion in Dawn's voice didn't pass unnoticed. "I'm often used by Angel Force as their key consultant on difficult cases. I'm hoping they won't have to call me in on this one, but it always helps to be prepared."

"I've seen you hanging out with Finn," Augustus said. "Do you really work with the angels?"

"All the time. They're thinking about dedicating a new wing to me and Zandra because we've been so helpful since we moved to Crimson Cove. Now, tell me about Hortense."

They exchanged a glance, then Augustus shrugged. "There's not much to say. She's not been here long, but she made her mark."

"Yeah. A big, unwelcome mark that hurts every time you prod it," Dawn said. "Hortense was bossy, stuck her opinion on things when it wasn't wanted, and thought she was in charge. She was no better than us. We all volunteer our time here because we love animals. But for some reason, she thought she was better than us."

"Hortense said she came from some important corporate place but retired early to give back to the community," Augustus said. "I just wish she hadn't picked this community to poke her spikey words into."

"She was grim to spend time with, but she knew how to put together a roster," Dawn said. "And Finn often asked her opinion on admin systems. He said she knew her stuff."

"Then he should have chained her to a desk and ensured she left us alone." Augustus smirked. "That would have been amusing."

"Was there anyone here she had a particular problem with?" I kept half an eye on Finn as he returned and talked to Zandra and Tia.

"I can't think of anyone whose nose she didn't put out of joint," Dawn said. "Hortense loved to make others miserable. I could never figure her out."

Augustus patted Dawn's arm. "I stayed out of her way whenever I could. It was the easiest way to deal with her."

"You let Hortense walk all over you." Dawn sighed. "I hate that I found her body, but I'm not sorry she's gone."

"You were the first to find her, weren't you?" I asked.

Dawn glanced at the barn and nodded. "Unfortunately. I was going in there to get fresh hay. I found her flat on the ground with that huge rake sticking out of her. It was so gross."

"Was there anyone else in there? Or did you see anyone leaving the scene?"

"No. I froze for a second, and the next thing I remember, I was screaming. I didn't even realize it was me screaming at first. Then you arrived, and everyone else came to see what was going on. Unless someone was hiding in the back, there was no one else in that barn when I got there."

I turned and looked at the barn. "Did she fight with anyone when she came back here after the bakery event?"

"If she did, we didn't see any fight," Augustus said. "And you always know when Hortense is arguing with someone. She gets louder and louder until they admit defeat."

There was a whoosh of air over my head, and Cythera arrived. She wasn't alone. Her handsome blond fiancé, Maverick, was with her.

"Thank you. If you'll excuse me." I hurried over to join the angels. They stood with Finn and Zandra. Tia had already left. "Cythera! This is hardly an appropriate date to bring your fiancé on."

She looked down at me. "Oh, goody. You're here."

"Always happy to help the less fortunate," I said. "Greetings, Maverick."

"Juno. It's a pleasure to see you again." He wore an open-necked red shirt and eye-wateringly tight dark denim jeans.

"If only it could be under happier circumstances."

"Yes, this is unfortunate. But when Cythera said she had a work emergency, I couldn't face leaving her, so I agreed to accompany her." Maverick beamed at me. "And I'm made of strong stuff. I can handle a crime scene."

"You came against my wishes." Cythera fluttered her wings in obvious annoyance. "Finn, show me what's going on."

I hopped onto Zandra's shoulder. "Did Tia have to leave?"

"She needed to get back to the bakery. Things to do. She seemed shocked about Hortense's death."

"I imagine she was," Maverick said. "This kind of work must require a cast iron constitution."

"I'm surprisingly used to it," I said. "Of course, when we found our first dead body—a headless corpse in a kitchen—it was a shock, but we soon recovered and saved the day. With the help of the angels, naturally."

Maverick appeared at a loss for what to say. He adjusted his wings and pressed a hand against his chest, as if checking to see if his heart still beat.

"Extraordinary. I couldn't do it. I work in public relations in the private sector. That's gruesome enough."

"You don't work for Angel Force?" I asked.

"Good heavens, what a thought. Public service isn't for me. There's no money in it, and I must be able to provide for my glorious fiancée."

"Cythera expects only the very best," Zandra said, not sounding the tiniest bit sarcastic.

"And I intend to give it to her. Whatever she desires, it'll be hers."

Cythera and Finn came out of the barn, and Finn closed the door. He didn't look happy when they returned to us.

"I'm not debating this anymore," Cythera said to him. "You were here at the time of the death, and you know the victim. You're too close to remain impartial."

"I don't know what happened to Hortense, though," Finn said. "I won't conceal things from you if I learn someone here did this. You can trust me."

"That's the end of the discussion. You're not working this case," Cythera said. "And you know there have been complaints about Hortense. Since it looks like this wasn't an accident, we must be careful to follow all protocols, and that means you aren't involved."

"This was murder?" Maverick asked.

Cythera ignored him. "We need to get everyone's details, and then this place must be cleared."

"We can help," I said. "You only have to ask. We offer reasonable rates."

"Stay out of this. I don't need your meddling. Finn, get to work," Cythera said. "Then go home and await my instructions."

"I have contact details for the volunteers in the office," Finn said. "And you know everyone else who's here."

Cythera gave me the stink eye. "Go. Now!" She strode off back to the barn and walked around it.

Maverick sighed. "What a woman. She has so much confidence and knows exactly what she's doing."

Since Cythera had rejected my offer of help, I decided to enjoy snooping into a different puzzle. "She is one of a kind. How well do you know Cythera?"

"I've known her most of my life." Maverick watched Cythera as she disappeared around the side of the barn.

"Childhood sweethearts?" Zandra asked.

"Not exactly. We were matched from a young age. Our families are one hundred percent angel. Purebloods, if you like. You know how nonsensical angels can be about matches, but it's important to our relations that we remain that way."

"So you don't get glorious misfit mixtures like Finn?" I narrowed my eyes. Was Maverick one of those disturbingly outdated genetic fanatics? If so, my fine opinion of him had just deflated.

"Don't get me wrong. I have nothing against angel hybrids, or any kind of hybrid, for that matter. We all have our place and purpose in this world. But some families are... traditional. Mine, in particular."

"It's not a love match?" I asked.

He considered my question. "It's a like match. But I worry about Cythera. This job consumes her."

"It's her passion," I said. "Why wouldn't she let it consume her when she enjoys it so much?"

"Perhaps you're right, but that'll all be over once we're married."

Zandra raised an eyebrow. "Cythera won't work when she's married to you?"

"She can work if she wants to, but why would she?" Maverick shuddered and glanced around at the gloom as the air chilled. "Heading out late at night to deal with a grisly death. No one would ever put that on their wish list."

"Cythera has her faults, but she has a strong head for justice. I can't imagine her being an angel of leisure," I said.

"When she sees what kind of life I can offer her, she'll resign in a heartbeat." Maverick nodded at us. "I must go check on my fiancée." He hurried off toward the barn, calling Cythera's name.

"Did I hear right?" Zandra muttered. "Maverick expects Cythera to give this up and run around after him like a good little housewife, shining his shoes and smiling all the time?"

I chuckled. "She'll hate that. She'll kill him."

"Cythera's in for some serious changes if this marriage takes place."

"Juno!" Binky bounded over, her expression one of panic.

"If you've heard about the body, don't worry. It wasn't Tia. She's already gone back to the bakery." I jumped off Zandra's shoulder and greeted Binky.

"It's not that. I know where Tia is, and I know she's safe. Can I have a minute? We need to talk." Binky trotted away, leaving me with no choice but to follow her.

"What's wrong?" I asked as I caught up with my anxious friend.

"This is bad. I'm worried. So is Tia." Binky made sure no one could hear us then paced in front of me.

"What's the problem?"

"The dead lady. The mean one who shouted at everyone. She's been arguing with Tia." Binky whined. "What should I do?"

"Calm yourself. Why is that a problem? From what I've heard, Hortense argued with everyone."

Binky dropped to the ground and covered her eyes with one giant paw. "During their last argument, Tia threatened to kill Hortense if she didn't leave her alone. And now..."

I rested a paw on Binky's head as she whimpered. "And now Hortense is dead. Oh, dear."

Chapter 5

Unwelcome suspect

"You haven't hung the pelt on the wall." I sat at the end of the bed as Zandra got dressed after showering.

"That thing isn't going anywhere near the wall. It's in the trash, where it belongs." She pulled on a pair of dark jeans and a lightweight sweater.

"It took hours to dig up! Give it a wash and it'll be a thing of beauty. My finest find. You must display it."

"No! And we have more important things to worry about than the rotting bit of dead animal you dragged into Vorana's house."

After yesterday's adventures at Finn's animal sanctuary, we'd headed home and gone to bed. I'd slept surprisingly well, considering one of my friends and her bonded magic user could be involved in Hortense's death. After Binky had expressed her worries about Tia, she'd raced away before I could grill her further, but I could tell she was worried Tia was in the middle of this murky murder and would do anything to protect her.

"I still can't get my head around Tia being involved," Zandra said.

"She isn't. I'm certain of it. Tia's been focused on getting the bakery reopened. Why would she spoil things by killing someone she barely knows?"

"Binky didn't say what the argument was about?" Zandra searched for her keys.

"She said it wasn't the first time they'd argued, but Tia would send Binky out whenever Hortense showed up, so she didn't have all the facts and didn't stick around long enough for me to ask probing questions. Binky must be digging for details, though. I would be if you were a murder suspect."

Zandra stood in the middle of the room, her hands on her hips as she looked around for her missing keys. "That doesn't sound good. But Hortense hasn't been in the area for long. The bakery reopening was the first time I'd met her."

"In that short time, she made a mark, and not a good one." I hopped off the bed, retrieved Zandra's keys from under the cabinet where she'd dropped them last night because she was so tired, and gifted them to her. "My only concern is Binky is fiercely loyal to Tia. She'd do anything to protect her."

Zandra raised her eyebrows. "You're thinking Binky is behind the murder? She was worried Hortense was causing trouble for Tia?"

"Not so much that, but what if an accident happened? Maybe Hortense pushed Tia too far. The hayfork would have been an easy weapon to grab if a fight broke out." I conjured the scene in my head but didn't like how it fit. "If Tia is involved, this'll get messy. Binky will protect Tia with her life, and she's quick to get snappy when she feels threatened."

"It won't come to that." Zandra shook her head. "We need to clear Tia's name before Cythera gets wind of what's going on. Make sure she has an airtight alibi."

"What we need to do is hurry. There's a mountain of food to get through at Finn's, and we've got an open breakfast invitation."

Zandra chuckled as we walked up the basement stairs. "Let's see how many day-old sausage sandwiches you can eat in one sitting."

Vorana and Sage were nowhere to be seen. Vorana had left early that morning to attend a book fair and wouldn't be back until late, so I was glad we'd received an invitation from Finn for breakfast. Zandra's idea of breakfast was cold cereal for her and dismal dried cat food for me. It was a less than acceptable start to the day.

We drove to the sanctuary in the work van and stopped beside a barn. I climbed out, the air alive with the sound of grumbling animals and stamping hooves, everyone impatient for their first meal. The barn where Hortense's body had been discovered was sealed off, but I doubted there was anything else to find in there. I'd had a good opportunity to look around the body, and other than the pungent meaty smell, there was nothing unusual about the scene.

Finn strode out of a nearby barn, raising his hand in greeting. "The coffee's brewing. Come to the office. I've got food in there, too."

"You look like you haven't slept." Zandra fell into step with him, and I followed a short way behind.

"Hardly a surprise. It's not every day you find a body in your barn." Finn opened the door and stepped back to let us in. "Any genius thoughts on what happened so we can get this case closed today?"

"A few. What do you think about Tia as a murder suspect?" I asked as we entered the tidy office with a small desk, chair, and piles of stacked folders.

"Unlikely. Why bring her name into this investigation?" Finn made the coffee and heaped plates with cold sausage sandwiches and chunks of pasty, which he passed around.

I kicked the top layer of pastry off my pasty and took a few bites of the meat. Not too herby but gristly. I'd expected more from Mystical Morsels. "Binky came to the sanctuary last night in a panic. She said Hortense and Tia had fought and things got tense. There may have been a minor death threat."

"From Tia? No way." Finn sipped his coffee. "What did they fight about?"

"No clue. Binky raced off before I could question her," I said. "But we're in agreement that Tia isn't involved. We can't lose her from Crimson Cove."

"Because you don't want to lose your supply of delicious bakery treats?" Zandra hid a smile behind her mug.

I sniffed. "That's one small reason. But we all like Tia. And Binky would be heartbroken if Tia was charged with Hortense's murder."

"Tia was here around the time the murder happened," Zandra said. "I'm not throwing her under the bus by saying that, but we can't rule her out until we've checked her alibi."

"Won't her alibi be Binky?" Finn asked. "And I know what you familiars are like. You'll do anything to keep your bonded magic user safe."

"That's true," I said. "When Zandra commits murder, I cover up the evidence and give her an airtight alibi, so no one even glances her way when the bodies show up. That's if they ever show up."

"That's barely even funny," Zandra said. "We need to make sure, when Cythera learns of Tia's issue with Hortense, she doesn't jump to the wrong conclusion. Cythera can be stubborn-headed when she latches onto a prime suspect and forgets the other candidates."

"I don't disagree." Finn drank more coffee. "The trouble is, I'm not on the case. Cythera made it clear I'm not to be involved with any part of the investigation. It's not fair! This happened at my animal sanctuary."

"Exactly, my friend. It's best you take a step back from this," I said.

A scowl crossed Finn's face, and he set down his mug. "Cythera suspects me. I know it."

"You! A murder suspect?" I chuckled. "What put that ludicrous idea into her feather-filled skull?"

He shrugged. "I made the mistake of grumbling about Hortense while I was at work."

"That's unlike you," Zandra said. "You like everyone. Even Bertoli."

Finn's laughter broke the lines of tension on his forehead. "Bertoli's not so bad. He's more chilled now he does regular meditation. Cythera is so impressed with him that she's sending him on sergeant's training. Some kind of intensive program so he can apply this year."

"He's a changed angel," I said. "He deserves a promotion."

"Yeah, I guess so. It's something I won't get anytime soon since I'm on the list of suspects. I won't be surprised if Cythera pulls me in for formal questioning today. She may even suspend me until the investigation is over."

"That's not so bad," Zandra said. "You were saying how busy you've been. You could spend the time getting things organized here, maybe get more volunteers trained, or figure out how to do things so you're less stressed."

Finn ran a hand through his hair. "I'm struggling to concentrate. There's so much going on. And I keep thinking about Hortense."

"Tell us more about her," I said. "I've heard a few rumors, but neither of us knew her."

He took a moment, his head tipped back as he stared at the ceiling. "The best word for Hortense is difficult. She was clever and quick to learn, but she was equally quick to point out people's flaws. That caused problems."

"For you?"

"For everyone. Hortense thought she was right about everything. And some of the time, she was. She helped me pull together a better volunteer roster and even negotiated a discount on feed for the animals. But she was tricky to handle. Even so, I considered her an asset to the sanctuary."

"What did she do that made you complain to Cythera?" Zandra asked.

"I didn't complain directly to Cythera, but I was talking to Bertoli about Hortense bossing me around and she overheard. It was hard to take. I've built this place up from nothing, and it's been a source of joy. But I stopped looking forward to coming here when Hortense was volunteering. The atmosphere was always so tense when she was around."

"If Cythera points the finger at you, you have the perfect alibi. You were with me," I said. "We must have been in the isolation barn for at least two hours healing those animals."

"I'm glad I was with you. Otherwise, I'd be in trouble. Any more pressure, and I'll pop." Finn shoved a chunk of pasty into his mouth. He chewed, grimaced, and removed something stringy. "Not loving these. I'll give them to the animals."

"Any feelings of paranoia today?" I asked.

Finn glanced at Zandra. "What do you mean?"

I finished my last bite of pasty and walked around the desk to sit in front of him. "Finn, you were hiding something yesterday. You were nervous, and you thought you were being watched. And you're still jumpy. You've always balanced the sanctuary and your job easily."

I waited for Finn to respond, but he stayed silent.

"I also sensed a dragon presence at the sanctuary. Does that have something to do with this pressure cooker environment?"

"Dragons!" Zandra exclaimed. "Why am I only just hearing about this?"

"Because Finn said it wasn't a problem. But I think there's something going on, isn't there? What aren't you telling us?"

He sat in a chair and rested his elbows on his knees. He was silent for a long time. "I've gotten in over my head, and I don't know how to fix it."

"Does this have to do with what happened to Hortense?" Zandra asked.

"No! At least, I don't think so. I'm not sure how she could have gotten involved with this or even learned about it. But she liked to poke around in places I didn't want her to. Maybe she figured things out." Finn lifted his head. "That wasn't a confession. I didn't kill her."

"What do you think she figured out?" I asked.

Finn drew in a slow breath. "I can trust both of you not to talk, right?"

"Of course," I said.

"So long as it's not something horrifically illegal you're hiding," Zandra said. "What have you gotten yourself into?"

"You can't tell anyone else about this," Finn said. "I'm serious. The more people who know, the more danger this will bring to Crimson Cove."

Zandra wrinkled her nose. "I'm not sure I want to know if it'll put me and Juno in danger."

"A little danger makes life thrilling," I said. "You can rely on us not to gossip to the uninformed."

Finn finished his coffee then stood. "Follow me. You need to see this to believe it."

I grabbed the piece of sausage Zandra tossed at me, then we followed Finn out of the office, passing the regular barns. We kept walking, crossing a small field until we reached a secure metal shed partially concealed by overhanging trees.

"Keep quiet," Finn whispered as he removed a barrier spell from in front of the shed and unlocked several large padlocks.

"What's in here?" Zandra said. "And how big are its teeth and claws?"

"Tiny at the moment." Finn pressed a finger to his lips. He eased open the door and gestured for us to follow him.

We crept inside a warm, slightly damp smelling shed. The damp wasn't a moldy type of damp. It felt more like I'd stepped inside a rainforest. There was a large pile of hay in one corner, and in the middle of that hay sat a huge dragon's egg. And there was a long crack running down one side.

My stomach tightened as I stared at the gently rocking egg, and my hackles lifted. "Finn, what have you done?"

He grimaced. "I know. The egg got left here ages ago, and I meant to find a suitable home for it, but things got busy, so I kept it here. Dragon eggs go dormant if they're not kept in the right conditions, so I figured I had plenty of time to find it a home. But then..."

"What happened?" Zandra asked. "You couldn't find a suitable adoptive family to take the egg?"

"I didn't look. I meant to. I just..." Finn lifted his hands. "Life got in the way. And I don't know why the dragon came out of hibernation, but one morning, I checked the egg, and it was warm! And then... the baby sang to me." His worried gaze lifted to meet Zandra's.

"You've bonded," I said. "Finn, that baby thinks you're its parent."

"I know! And I didn't mean for this to happen. I meant to get this egg to a suitable family so they could raise the baby."

"Finn, you're an idiot," Zandra said. "Of course, the baby would want to bond with you. You'll make a perfect dad. You're loyal, friendly, and loving. Any child raised by you will be happy."

He grinned. "You think I'd make a good dad?"

I swatted his leg with a paw. "Focus! This can't happen. Dragons must be raised by their own kind, or they become dangerous. A dragon who isn't raised with other dragons will never learn to control their incredible power and strength. If you keep it and it hatches, it'll have to be destroyed. You know the rules."

Finn crossed his arms over his chest. "It's too late now. We have a connection. If I let this baby go, she'll die. I can't do that to her."

"It's a girl?" Zandra said.

"I... yeah, I think so. I've been spending a lot of time with her. She sings to me all the time. It's so beautiful. Her song haunts my dreams."

"Dragon's song is hypnotic. And by the looks of that crack, she's about to come out," I said.

"No, it'll be a while. She's not ready yet. She told me, but she's getting there." Finn stood in front of the egg. "I can handle this. I know I can."

"Even though yesterday you were telling us you can't cope with everything you've already got on your plate?" I swatted him again. "Add in a hatchling and your life will go ka-boom. And so will Crimson

Cove when that dragon loses control." I liked dragons well enough, but I'd witnessed enough ill-mannered ones to know they had to be handled with extreme caution.

Finn rubbed his forehead with the tips of his fingers. "I know it's a lot. I also know I've made a huge mistake, but I'm dealing with it. Please, don't tell anyone about her. I haven't worked out the fine details yet, but I will."

"You're going to get yourself killed," I said.

"Not by the baby," Finn said. "She trusts me."

I sighed. Finn wasn't usually this naïve when dealing with magical creatures. "I wasn't thinking about the baby. I was thinking about—"

Cythera's voice interrupted us from outside the barn. "Finn, where are you? We need to talk."

Chapter 6

Secret da-da

Finn's eyes widened as he lunged at the egg. "Cythera can't find the dragon. She'll fire me and have me arrested. Don't let her in."

"Technically, you have broken some serious laws," I said. "Maybe she needs to know."

"Juno! Now's not the time to mess around." Zandra was already by the door, holding it shut. "Put up the barrier spell. If we stay silent, she may go away."

"I can hear you. And I'm going nowhere. What are you doing in there?" Cythera rattled the handle.

"Give me a second. And don't come in. There's a wounded animal. It may turn aggressive if it sees an unfamiliar face," Finn yelled.

"Hurry! We need to talk about what happened yesterday."

"Go outside. Distract her for me. Please," Finn pleaded.

"Leave it to us. I'll go outside. I just need a small gap to squeeze through. You deal with Finn and his egg," I said to Zandra.

"Shush. Cythera can't suspect anything." Finn piled straw over the egg in a desperate attempt to hide it.

I squeezed through the gap in the open door and hurried over to Cythera, who was scowling. No surprise there. "Greetings! It's wonderful to see you. Have you done something new with your hair?"

Her scowl deepened. "What are you all doing in there? And what type of animal is Finn dealing with? I hope he has the correct license to handle a dangerous beast."

"I'm sure he does. Finn always does the right thing."

"Perhaps I should help if he's having trouble." Cythera stepped around me, but I blocked her path.

"The beastie has an upset stomach. It's a mess in there, and it stinks. There are piles of—"

"I don't need to know any more." She pulled a face of disgust and made no more attempts to get past me.

I relaxed a fraction. "How's it going with the murder investigation? Any suspects yet?"

Cythera rolled her eyes. "I suppose it's no surprise you're poking around in this investigation."

"Always happy to poke. And I was here when Hortense died, so I'm crucial to your investigation."

"That's true. What were you doing when the victim was murdered?"

I hissed out my surprise. "Not killing her!"

"Hey, Cythera. Juno was with me." Finn stepped out of the shed, followed by Zandra. "I didn't expect to see you here this morning. It's early."

"I'm here to question you before your shift starts," she said. "In private."

"You can say anything you like in front of Juno and Zandra," he replied. "I've got no secrets."

The dragon egg-sized secret in the shed suggested otherwise, but I kept my mouth shut about that.

"Very well. I spent last night talking to your volunteers," Cythera said. "There was mention there'd been disagreements between you and Hortense. Tell me more. Was there a problem between you?"

"You already know I wasn't her biggest fan." Finn walked away from the shed. "Hortense was prickly. She spoke her mind, and what was on her mind wasn't always pleasant."

"You didn't like her?" Cythera followed.

"I appreciated her hard work, but I was thinking she wasn't the best fit for the sanctuary. I want this place full of calm, positive energy. The vibes a person gives off affect the animals."

"Have you noticed how Finn's rescue critters often run away from you?" I asked Cythera.

She flared her wings. "It's my size. It intimidates them."

Finn bit his lip to trap in a grin. "Sometimes, the animals got skittish around Hortense. I tried to keep her in the office as much as possible, but she liked being outside. She said she needed a change from her old job."

"You wanted to get rid of her?" Cythera asked.

"I didn't say that. Not in so many words, but it was on my mind. Hortense was incredible at doing admin. She helped make this place run smoothly, so I didn't want to let her go, but I thought I might have to find her another role. One that limited her interaction with people."

I sidled closer to Finn. "How did Hortense get involved in the sanctuary?"

"She showed up at an open day for volunteers. She filled in a form, and I interviewed her like I do with everyone, and we decided to give it a try. This place has been expanding, and I need more capable helping hands."

Cythera's mouth twisted. "I'm aware you often leave early from the job you're actually paid to do."

"Hey! It's only been three times I've had to leave early in the last year, and that was when there was an emergency. And you approved it because the request came from animal control. Barney needed help."

"Finn's an asset to the community," I said. "The town would be overrun with out-of-control creatures if it weren't for him."

"Is that so? Isn't that your job?" Cythera asked.

I held in a sigh. "What I'm saying is, you shouldn't chastise Finn for doing good work. And before you continue to grill him like he's the prime suspect, we were together for two hours before Hortense died. We were in the isolation barn, performing healing magic. I'm happy to testify that truth to anyone."

Cythera snorted softly, her attention remaining on Finn. "I'm still not happy there was bad blood between you and Hortense."

"As much as I'm not a fan of coincidences," I said, "this is one of them. It was unfortunate that whoever got rid of Hortense did it here."

"They must have seen the opportunity and grabbed it," Zandra said.

Cythera grumbled to herself but made no more allegations to suggest she thought Finn was the murderer.

"Since I have a rock-solid alibi," Finn said, "can I get in on the case?"

"No, that's not possible. You were too close to the victim. You won't be able to remain impartial."

"What other suspects are you pursuing?" I asked Cythera.

"There are a few names that have risen to the top of my list."

"And they are?"

"If I need your involvement, I'll let you know."

I glanced at Zandra. "Anyone local?"

I got silence.

"Is that a yes?"

"It seems you already know I'm interested in a certain baker." Cythera wheeled on me. "What can you tell me about Tia's involvement?"

"It wasn't her. She's innocent."

"I don't disagree with you."

Her response caught me by surprise. "She's not a suspect?"

"Tia is no longer a person of interest."

"But..."

Cythera huffed out a breath. "Tia isn't the problem. But Binky has been confined to a cell."

"You think Binky killed Hortense?" Zandra said. "Do you have any evidence?"

Cythera crossed her arms. "Did I hire you to investigate this case?"

"Um... no. But we could help. What have you got on Binky that's put her in a cell?"

"There's nothing to help with, so you don't need me to provide you with additional information."

"How would Binky have been able to stab Hortense with the hayfork? Having paws makes it tricky to be dexterous. It takes practice. If only we had opposable thumbs." I studied my front paws.

"What have you got on Binky?" Finn asked when Cythera didn't answer my question.

Cythera's sigh suggested we were wasting her time. "Binky became aggressive when we questioned her. She threatened to eat my angels."

I stifled a laugh. "An angel would be a tasty treat for a cougar familiar. You always smell like sugar-spun candy."

"This isn't a joking matter. She almost pounced on one of them! I had to restrain her."

"Were you questioning Tia when things got tense?" I asked. "Exactly how vigorous was your interrogation?"

"It wasn't an interrogation. I know how to conduct a professional interview. Nothing untoward took place, so there was no reason for Binky to become aggressive."

"Cythera, as adorable as you are, you're not known for your tact," I said. "Binky could have misinterpreted what you were saying to Tia. She may have thought you meant Tia harm. It was natural for her to protect her bonded magic user."

"I'd never harm a murder suspect," Cythera said. "I'd charge them and put them behind bars, but that would be it."

"What about the other angels involved?" I asked. "Did they do anything shady?"

"I don't recruit shady angels!" Cythera adjusted her wings, pulling out a stray feather.

"But..." Finn prodded. "Something went wrong that triggered Binky?"

Cythera stopped preening. "One of my new recruits was nervous. They could have been flaring their wings. But that didn't give Binky the right to attack."

"I'd attack a twitchy angel if she came at me with a bad attitude and her wings out," I said.

"Then you'd be behind bars too," Cythera said. "Binky is dangerous and unstable. Or have you forgotten her past?"

"That's unfair. She's a reformed character. It wasn't Binky's choice to be stolen and used by a dark magic user. Binky is innocent, just like Tia."

"I'm still deciding if that's true," Cythera said. "But Binky broke the law. We can't allow familiars to think it's acceptable to threaten angels."

I sat back on my haunches. "You seem tense. Is the wedding stress getting to you?"

"Juno, not now," Zandra muttered.

"You have no idea," Cythera replied.

"I could assist. I've attended plenty of stunning weddings. Perhaps I could give you ideas for decorations or unusual flavors of wedding cake."

"Stay out of my private life," Cythera growled at me.

I ignored the warning. "Maverick is charming. I approve of your match, as long as he makes you happy."

She jabbed a finger at me. "If you don't shut that fluffy mouth, I'll put you in the same cell as Binky. And I'll lose the key."

I lifted a paw in recognition I'd pushed this angel too far. "I'm just saying you have friends who want to support you. Maverick has told us about how your union came to be. That must add a layer of complication. If you need to talk..."

She bared her teeth. "I'll have words with my fiancé and tell him not to talk to anyone but a select few. This is a personal matter between me and him. It needs no outside interference."

"Juno is trying to help." Finn flashed me a warning look. "But I agree with her. Maverick seems like a decent guy. You could do a lot worse."

"Let's talk about the case in private, with no more unwanted interference." Cythera turned and strode away without a backward glance.

"You may have gone too far this time," Finn said to me. "I'll be back soon." He hurried after Cythera.

"Cythera is out of her mind for shoving Binky in a cell," I said. "Tia will be frantic. Binky doesn't do well on her own. Not since she got stolen and messed with by dark power. It left her fragile."

"Tia will be getting Binky out as we speak." Zandra lifted me onto her shoulder. "You need to watch your step around Cythera. She's got serious pre-wedding jitters, and poking at her will make things worse. She'll shut us out of this case completely if we're not careful."

"My offer of assistance was genuine. But perhaps you're right. The angels are so odd when finding their forever mates."

"Let's focus on the murder, not matrimonial meddling."

I sat for a moment while Finn and Cythera talked in earnest, out of our earshot. "There are more obvious suspects for the angels to focus on."

"We agree it wasn't Finn, nor Binky and Tia, so we can rule them out. Who are you thinking?" Zandra asked.

"The night Hortense was killed, I overheard two sanctuary volunteers, Dawn and Augustus, gossiping about her. I asked them a few questions, and I learned she was unpopular."

"No surprise there. Was Dawn the one who found Hortense?"

"That's right."

"She seemed shocked, but she didn't appear to be upset. They didn't like each other?"

"Dawn wasn't sad about the murder. And when I was listening in to their conversation, they were talking about karma giving Hortense what she deserved. They were open about their dislike of her."

"So, it could have been one of them who killed her?" Zandra asked.

"Dawn was on the scene first, so we need to talk to her. And Augustus, too."

"What about the camera guy?" Zandra said. "Hortense kept hassling him at the opening event.

I even saw her shove him. And she wasn't happy he was filming at the sanctuary last night."

"You think he had a grudge against her because of that?"

"Maybe. I overheard him say Hortense almost broke some of his equipment."

"It's a motive of sorts. I know how weird tech geeks get with their gadgets. Randal gets super strange when I tinker with his new toys."

Zandra smirked. "Let's stick to the suspects, shall we?"

"In a moment. You never told me how your date went."

"What date?" She sighed when I remained silent. "It got cut short because we found a dead body. Murder trumps romance."

"Ah, good point. We'll have to try again."

"I'm not so sure. Every time we try to date, something gets in the way. Maybe this is karma giving me a nudge and telling me not to bother with Randal."

"Karma wouldn't do that. You're talking about fate. Two very different beasts. Fate has put you and Randal in the same place, and it's clear you like each other. Fate wants you to see if you can overcome the hurdles and get to your happily ever after."

"Why must there be hurdles?" Zandra blew a raspberry. "I'm not sure I even believe in fate. If I do, I want words with her. She's way too complicated for me to figure out."

Finn returned from talking to Cythera. She didn't join him and instead took to the wing and vanished.

"Bad news?" I asked him.

"It's not terrible news. Cythera's willing to share a few details about the case, now she knows my alibi," Finn said.

"What did she tell you?" Zandra asked.

"They've done a prelim autopsy on Hortense's body, and they don't think the cause of death was the hayfork stuck in her chest."

"It looked fatal to me," Zandra said.

"A meat pasty was lodged in her throat," Finn said. "Cythera thinks she choked to death then was stabbed with the hayfork."

"The meat smell!" I said. "When I was looking around Hortense's body, I smelled something pungent. And she had crumbs on her face and shoulders. She was eating when attacked?"

"Cythera thinks whoever killed her forced that food into her mouth."

"Her killer choked her with the pasty and then stabbed her with the hayfork to ensure she didn't get back up?" Zandra said. "Wow! Someone really wanted Hortense dead."

Finn nodded. "It looks like it."

"Does Cythera seriously think Tia or Binky were involved?" I asked.

"No, but she's being stubborn because Binky behaved badly. She put Binky in the cells to teach her a lesson."

"I knew it," I said. "It's the wedding stress making Cythera behave like this. We should get involved with the planning. I know some wonderful caterers. Anything to take the strain off so we avoid being angel whipped."

"Do not go meddling in that wedding," Zandra said. "And stop stirring. No more wedding questions. Besides, we won't get an invitation, so if you help, you won't see the end result."

"Oh, you will," Finn said. "Maverick is determined to invite all of Cythera's friends to the ceremony and the meal afterward. Have you ever been to an angel wedding?"

"Several. They're fabulous," I said. "Lots of color, flowers, feathers, and food. Although the ceremony goes on for hours. We'll need snacks so we can power through without dozing off."

"I've heard about them," Zandra said. "If I get an invitation, will I have to wear white?"

Finn grinned. "Just you wait. It'll be a day you'll never forget."

"So, what's Cythera doing next to find out what happened to Hortense?" I asked. "Who's her next target?"

"She wouldn't tell me, but she was planning on amusing herself by taking her time over Binky's release paperwork. Once Binky has suitably stewed, she'll sign it off and let her go. Cythera thinks that'll teach Binky a lesson."

I shook my head. "That's unacceptable. We need to solve this. No one mistreats our friends and gets away with it."

"What do you suggest we do?" Zandra said.

"It's time to get sleuthing. And I know where to start."

Chapter 7

Secret sleuthing

After a morning at animal control and a quick check on Sammy before he left for his rehab, we snuck to Angel Force and waited outside for Finn. We didn't want Cythera seeing us together and learn we were interfering in an investigation she told us to keep out of. We were also on the hunt for an escaped red spotted panda cub, so we figured we'd multi-task by searching for the critter while we snooped.

Finn emerged ten minutes later. He strolled along the street, passing by the alleyway where we'd hidden ourselves. "You're good. Cythera is in a meeting so she won't see us together."

Zandra handed him an enchanted net. "Use this if you see our escapee. The panda looks cute, but they have huge fangs."

"And their saliva immobilizes you," I said.

He gripped the net, his gaze darting around. "Got it. Look out for the adorable killer panda that spits and wants to tear my head off."

"How's the investigation progressing?" I hopped onto Zandra's shoulder as she joined Finn, and we started our walk-hunt-snoop mission.

"Tia and Binky are in the clear, and it definitely wasn't me," Finn said. "So that's three suspects crossed off the list."

"We were thinking it could be the gossiping volunteers I met last night," I said. "Tell us more about Dawn and Augustus."

"You know them?" Finn asked.

"I met them at your sanctuary. They didn't have nice things to say about Hortense." I directed Zandra toward a large pile of moving trash that awaited collection. Something squirmed beneath one bag.

"Hortense often picked on the younger volunteers. I got the impression she thought she could bend them to her will more easily than my seasoned volunteers." Finn raised his net as Zandra kicked aside the bag. No panda cub.

"From what I saw of Dawn and Hortense at the bakery reopening, that plan didn't work out so well for her," Zandra said. "She wasn't afraid to stand up to Hortense when she bossed her around."

"True. Those two have had their disagreements." Finn paused to inspect a window display of ties in the thrift store. "Dawn Summer is a fae-human. She's twenty, a college dropout, and loves animals. She had a rough start in life. She was referred to the sanctuary through her social worker."

"You took her in?" Zandra asked.

"Kinda. They placed her in three different organizations, but she only lasted a few months in each. Then she vanished, and they were worried something bad had happened to her."

"You found Dawn on your own?" I prodded Zandra to head along an alley behind the stores. Baby red spotted pandas liked quiet, dark holes.

"I've got connections in social services, and one of my friends was talking about Dawn going missing and them fearing the worst. I did some informal asking around, and I found her hanging out in the rough part of town. I convinced her to give the animal sanctuary a try."

"For a half-demon, you have a soft heart," I said.

Finn grinned as he used his enchanted net to check inside a discarded cardboard box. "It took work. Dawn isn't trusting, although you can't blame her after everything she's been through. She's been let down more than a handful of times. She can be argumentative, too. But I figured she needed a chance. And she's great with the animals. They respond well to her."

"Where does she live?" Zandra asked.

"She's staying at the sanctuary. It's all above board. I've got a couple of rooms set aside so people can stay overnight to care for the animals that need intensive support. It's a temporary thing, but it's working out great, and Dawn is always around if any animal needs her."

"Does she have a criminal past?" I asked.

"She's gotten into a few scrapes. Minor stuff, like stealing food or clothing. The sort of thing you do when you're desperate rather than a bad apple."

"If Dawn has a temper, she must have clashed with Hortense regularly." Zandra stooped and inspected animal scat. It was fresh. Could be from our escapee.

"Oh, they clashed. But I'm not sure that's enough of a motive for Dawn to kill Hortense. They were always bickering. That was how they handled their relationship," Finn replied.

"We'll need to talk to her," I said. "Check her movements."

"Cythera has already spoken to the volunteers who were there, and she has Dawn's alibi on record," Finn said. "I can check the notes."

"We'll have an informal chat with Dawn, too. She may be more open to a less formal style of questioning," I said.

"So long as Cythera doesn't catch you snooping, it's fine by me," Finn said. "Tell Dawn I said it was okay to talk to you if she's suspicious. And don't take it personally if she shuts down. She's mistrustful of everyone to begin with."

"What about the other volunteer?" I asked. "Dawn was talking to a guy with a long beard just after Hortense died."

"Augustus Wellington. He's a new guy. He seems nice. Pretty quiet."

"How did he get involved in the sanctuary?" Zandra inched along the alley.

"He showed up at the same recruitment day as Hortense. I don't know much about him. He takes his orders and ambles off to do what I ask. It's kind of perfect. He never asks questions, shows up when he's needed, and gets things done."

"What about his background? Anything that causes you concern?" I asked.

"He's got no criminal record. Augustus seems like a drifter, doesn't put down roots, won't stay anywhere too long. And I could only speak to one of his referees. All volunteers provide either employment or character references. The guy I spoke to said positive things, but I couldn't get hold of the other one. Apparently, he's on a silent retreat, so no one can contact him."

"Does that concern you?" I said. "Perhaps Augustus lied about one of his referees for a reason."

"I've been meaning to follow it up, but I've been so busy. I'm not concerned, though. And he's triggered no alarm bells with his behavior. He's polite, respectful, and does what he's told."

"Did Augustus spend much time with Hortense?" Zandra inspected scratch marks on the wall and a small piece of fur and nodded. More clues that our panda cub had been here.

"They hung out occasionally, but I wouldn't have called them friends. Hortense didn't make friends." Finn also inspected the scratch marks. "Is there anyone else you consider a suspect from what you saw at the bakery opening?"

"Hortense got feisty with a camera operator," I said. "Do you know anything about him?"

"Percival Thornfield." Finn turned from the wall. "He seems like a good guy. Pushy with the camera, constantly filming when you don't realize it, so he catches you fooling about or stuffing your face with food, but he's passionate about his work."

"Hortense didn't like him."

"It was more a case of her being protective of the sanctuary," Finn said. "Hortense told me she was worried Percival was trying to find some angle so he could do an expose on the place. He works freelance, so he is always looking for stories to sell. And scandal sells better than happily ever afters."

I glanced around, but there was no one in the alley to overhear us. "Was Percival hoping to expose the dragon egg you've got hidden? Maybe he's heard whispers and wanted to get to the truth."

Finn grimaced. "No one needs to hear about that. I'd get in so much trouble. But he can't know about my baby. No one does."

"We do." Zandra arched an eyebrow at Finn.

He raised his net. "Yeah, but I trust you not to blab to the wrong people."

"We should talk with Percival, too," I said. "He could have held a grudge against Hortense for her bad behavior. When he was filming at the bakery opening, she was rough on him."

"Anyone else?" Zandra tilted her head as a soft scuffling sound drifted from the end of the alley.

"The suspect list is wide open if you want to add names." Finn crouched and edged closer to the sound.

"Gently," I whispered. "And watch out for panda spit balls."

"Gross." Finn tiptoed closer to a pile of trash. He flipped a bag with his foot and lunged, his net swooping down. He lost his balance and crashed behind the bags. There was a startled mewl then silence.

"You good?" Zandra peered over the top of the boxes.

Finn was on his back. He clutched the squirming baby to his chest as it clawed and hissed. "Got it! This baby stinks!"

"He was in the yard for bath time when he took offense and ran off. His owner has been reminded of her responsibilities," I said. "Behave, youngster, or you'll be shackled."

The infant lobbed a gooey spitball my way. Ungrateful baby.

After a few minutes of wrangling and several near misses with panda spitballs, we emerged from the alley, victorious and sweaty. The baby red spotted panda didn't share in our victory dance.

A smiling woman crossed the road to join us. I recognized her from last night's sanctuary event. "It's Finn, isn't it? I'm Celeste Hearthstone. We met yesterday."

Finn stopped dancing. "Of course. I remember." He held out his hand for her to shake then retracted it. "Sorry, I don't smell so sweet. Our badly behaving escapee needs a shower. And now, so do I."

"How adorable." Celeste crouched to peer at the infant, who was held in restraints by Zandra's side.

"I'd advise caution unless you want globs of panda spit on your dress," I said.

"Oh! Of course." She eyeballed the captive then stepped back. "Cute but deadly, huh?"

Finn smiled warmly at Celeste. "I didn't know you were still in Crimson Cove."

"We planned to leave after the bakery opening and once we'd secured enough footage of the local area to put together a report, but after what happened at your sanctuary, we stayed."

"There's no story, if that's what you're looking for." My hackles lifted. "What happened to Hortense was a tragedy."

"Oh, don't misunderstand me," Celeste said. "It's an absolute tragedy, but we wanted to see if there was anything we could do."

"To help Hortense, you mean?" Finn asked.

"Actually, the general area. I was thrilled to form this partnership with Gingerbread Bakery. We have similar deals all over the country, and this was a perfect fit. And when we establish a partnership in a town, we look for local causes to support." Celeste's smile brightened. "Which is why I'm glad I ran into you."

"If you're thinking of supporting Finn's animal sanctuary, you couldn't pick a better place," I said. "He takes the best care of them. The animals give him a five-star rating when they leave to go to their new homes."

Celeste nodded. "I was impressed when I visited. Everyone I spoke to had nothing but praise for Finn's work. You're a local hero."

Finn blushed. "I wouldn't say that. I'm doing it for selfish reasons. I get pleasure out of helping the animals."

"Modest too. The dream package," Celeste said. "I'd be honored if the company could support the sanctuary with donations of food and equipment. We also have a grant program, so we make financial donations too."

"You have? I mean, that's amazing. It would help so much. I never meant for the sanctuary to get this big, but I can never turn away an animal in need," Finn said.

"All I need in return is positive publicity and a few pictures now and again. Nothing onerous. I'm aware organizations such as yours run on a shoestring budget, so you don't want to be bogged down by paperwork. What do you say to a partnership with Mystical Morsels?"

"I say yes!"

"And hopefully, it'll make up for the tragic death. It's all I've heard people talk about since I've been here. That poor woman." Celeste shook her head.

"Did you know her?" I asked.

"I saw her at the bakery opening, and we spoke briefly, but that was it. I'm glad I can sprinkle positivity over everything that's gone on."

"Keep spreading it," Finn said. "Sprinkle as much as you like. What do we do next? How soon can the donations start?"

Celeste chuckled. "I'll have my office contact you. There's paperwork to fill in, nothing too lengthy, and then I'll send a camera crew to film and do interviews."

"Finn is the perfect poster boy. He won't let you down," I said.

"I agree. It was wonderful to see you again." Celeste nodded goodbye and strode away.

"Lucky you," Zandra said to Finn. "Your prayers have been answered."

"I wondered why Celeste was spending so much time at the sanctuary talking to people," Finn said.

"She must have been looking into the place to see if we were worth supporting."

"Now you have a patron, you'll be under less pressure," I said. "You could hire that assistant we were talking about."

"Yeah, there's a lot to think about." Finn checked the time. "I need to get back to work. Cythera will ask questions if I'm not around when she comes out of her meeting."

"Is Dawn volunteering at the sanctuary today?" I asked.

Finn nodded. "She's always there."

"Then we'll speak to her later."

"Great. I'll catch up with you as soon as I can." Finn hurried away.

"And make sure Binky's been released," I called after him.

"Already on it." He lifted a hand.

The panda lobbed a spitball at him.

"Enough of that! Let's get you home, bathed, and put to bed, where you can think about your bad manners and where they got you." I waggled a paw at the naughty youngster.

Zandra laughed. "This baby reminds me of you when we first met."

"I never spat!"

"You cursed and threw dark spells around like they were confetti."

I sniffed her ear. "We've both come a long way since that encounter. Let's deal with this baby then we'll figure out how to grill Dawn."

We'd also returned to work after catching up with Finn but had gotten away early and headed straight to the animal sanctuary to speak to Dawn.

"We need to handle her gently," I said. "From Finn's description, she's skittish, so we don't want her clamming up and not answering our questions."

"I'll let you handle the questioning, then," Zandra said.

I chortled. Zandra could be blunt when getting information from people, but at least she knew it and would step out of the way rather than putting her booted foot into things that needed a delicate tread.

After we'd parked the van, we spent ten minutes wandering around in search of Dawn. We found her moving boxes out of a storeroom. Her pale green eyes narrowed as we approached, but she relaxed when she recognized us.

"If you're looking for Finn, he's not here," she said.

"Greetings! We're here to speak to you," I said. "We met last night. And this is my wonderful witch, Zandra Crypt."

"Sure, I know who you are. You're always hanging out with Finn."

"We consider him a friend," I said. "He was telling us you've been staying here."

"What if I have?"

"We have no problem with that. But after what happened to Hortense, we hoped you might help us figure out how she died. You were the first on the scene."

"Oh, that." Dawn turned away and set down the boxes. "The angels have already questioned me.

They know everything, not that I had much to tell them."

"We're working with Angel Force," I said. "And we don't want the sanctuary getting a bad reputation."

"Why would this affect the sanctuary?"

"People may be scared to visit. It could mean Finn gets fewer donations if word gets out there's a killer on the loose and targeting people here."

"They're not! I mean, it was only Hortense who died."

"Only Hortense?" Zandra said.

Dawn sighed. "I didn't mean it like that. But you must have seen how she operates. She was a dragon."

"I noticed she disagreed with a few people," I said.

"Not me. I kept out of her way. I don't look for hassle. I keep my head down and my nose clean."

"You never argued with Hortense?"

"She wasn't worth my time."

"So, you didn't argue with her yesterday at the bakery opening?" I asked.

Dawn stared at me for an uncomfortable amount of time. "I wouldn't have called that an argument. I just didn't let her push me around. If she shoved me, I shoved back. It was how we rolled."

"And you weren't gossiping about Hortense after you found her body in the barn?"

"I wouldn't waste my breath gossiping about that shrew."

"And yet you did. Because I overheard you."

"I knew you were listening to us!" Dawn said. "I told Augustus you were snooping when you came over. What was Hortense to you?"

"I'm curious about her. And I was snooping because I was concerned about you. You just found a body. That's not a memory that leaves you feeling tingly and happy."

Dawn shrugged. "It wouldn't be my first body."

"What do you mean?" Zandra asked.

Dawn flipped open the lid of a box. "I should get on."

"We're interested," I said.

She was quiet as she checked through the contents of the box. "I didn't have it so good growing up. I saw things. I spent time on the streets, and there are nasty things out there. And just because we have magic doesn't mean we get a fairytale life."

"But then Finn helped you," I said.

A faint smile flickered across Dawn's sharp face. "He's one of the good ones. I wasn't sure about him at first, figured he was a wing-flapping do-gooder, but he's been decent. He gets that I prefer animals to people and doesn't hassle me."

"Don't we all," Zandra said. "Did you have a problem with Hortense?"

"Sure. But it wasn't what you think."

I flicked an ear. "You don't know what we're thinking."

"Sure, I do. You think I had something to do with what happened to her. I found her, so I'm involved. I'm not." Dawn turned away. "I... I've been flirting with Finn, and Hortense got jealous. She didn't like him paying me more attention than her."

I twitched my ears again. I hadn't expected that. Dawn was a little young for Finn.

"Did Hortense warn you off?" Zandra said.

"She wasn't that direct, but she hated it. I could tell by the way she watched me. It creeped me out, but I didn't stop flirting. And when she kept nagging me, I knew the reason."

"Was Hortense also interested in Finn?" I asked.

"She must have been. Or maybe she didn't like seeing us happy. It's fun to flirt with Finn."

"He does give good flirt," Zandra said.

"Not to Hortense. And she loathed that." Dawn shifted her attention to another box. "I shouldn't have gossiped about Hortense, but I had nothing to do with her death. She was annoying and kept trying to take over, but she didn't own this place, and I was glad to tell her that as often as I had to before it sunk in."

A thunder-like rumble rolled around us, and the air crackled with magic.

"Not again," Dawn said. "These weird sounds keep happening, and it makes everyone nervous, Finn included. When I asked him about it, he told me it was nothing to worry about, just magic interfering with the town border spells."

Zandra cocked her head, looking at the sky. "That wasn't thunder, was it?"

"I don't think so," I muttered. "I have an idea what it could be. Dawn, I hope you don't mind me asking, but what were you doing last night at the sanctuary? How did you come to discover Hortense's body?"

She threw up her hands. "After everything I've told you, you still think I'm guilty?"

"No. But we need to establish alibis for everyone who was there."

Her face grew pinched as she glowered at me. "You were there. Are you suspects?"

"We have alibis," I said.

"I've already told the angels."

"Tell us too. Then we'll leave you alone."

"Waste of time," she mumbled. "I was working with Augustus, feeding the animals in the end barn, where they have the cats and those stinky musk rats with wings. I went to the food barn to get some pellets. That was when I found Hortense."

"Thanks. We appreciate your help," I said.

"Yeah, whatever." Dawn lifted her chin, her gaze drifting past us. "Finn's here. And I've got things to do."

Finn approached the barn, but Dawn didn't stick around to greet him. Instead, she hurried into a nearby store and shut the door with a firm thud.

"Good news. Binky's been released with no charges," Finn said.

"Tia will be relieved," I replied.

Zandra gestured with her head, and we walked away from the storeroom so Dawn wouldn't overhear us.

"How'd you get on?" Finn kept his voice low. "Did Dawn talk to you?"

"She was prickly but gave us a decent alibi, and it'll be easy to check," Zandra said.

"I looked at the transcript from her interview. Did Dawn say she was with Augustus?"

I nodded.

"Then she's in the clear," Finn said. "I'm glad. She's a great volunteer."

"Finn, wait up." Torrin Conner walked through the barn gates and hurried toward us. He was a short, stocky half-dragon with red scales on his arms and an impressive set of muscles.

"Hey. What's up?" Finn's smile faded as Torrin got closer, his steps rapid and shoulders tight.

Torrin's dark eyes flashed with concern. "Bro, we have a serious problem."

Chapter 8

Fiery clue

"Torrin didn't say what the problem was?" Vorana served up plates of beef pot pie and creamed potato.

"Finn joked it was guy stuff, and we wouldn't be interested in what Torrin had to say." I nudged Sage with a paw to get her to move the smoked salmon entrée we'd been given closer. I didn't want her to hog it down before I'd had my portion.

"And Torrin got grumpy when we didn't leave," Zandra said. "He even blew smoke from his nose."

"Finn reckoned it was Torrin's hormones playing up, but they didn't want to share their gossip," I said.

"Typical men," Sorcha Creer said. She'd been having dinner with us at least three times a week since she'd ditched her deceitful boyfriend. "They keep secrets. You can't trust them. They have hidden agendas."

"You can trust Finn and Torrin." Vorana took her seat at the table in her kitchen after everyone had been served. "We've been friends with them for a long time."

"Finn is an outrageous flirt, and Torrin has a fiery temper. You need to watch them for bad behavior," Sorcha said. "They're not perfect."

"Who is?" Zandra took a bite of food and nodded her approval at Vorana.

"It's true," I said. "Zandra is known for being stubborn and having temper issues. Vorana can be so focused on making other people happy, she exhausts herself. Sorcha can never say no to a lost cause. And Sage is known for her curmudgeonly nature."

They all stared at me.

"What about you?" Sage said. "You're Little Miss Paw-fect?"

I considered my few flaws. "I never walk away from a challenge."

"That's hardly a character flaw." Zandra rolled her eyes.

"You hide stuff," Sage said.

I jabbed her with a paw. The less she said about my hiding stuff, the better.

"Perhaps Finn and Torrin wanted to talk about Hortense's murder," Vorana said.

"Why would that need keeping a secret?" Sorcha asked.

"Finn was initially a suspect," I said. "And Dawn mentioned she'd flirted with Finn, so he could have been worried he'd overstepped and would get in trouble, so he was seeking a guy's point of view."

"Dawn's a suspect?" Vorana filled her water glass from a pitcher on the table.

Zandra nodded. "There are a few. Dawn found Hortense's body."

"How terrible. How old is she?"

"Twenty. Dawn's not afraid of confrontation, though. That's why we were interested in her," I said.

"Finn probably thought she was an easy mark. Or he went on an ego boost and let Dawn flirt and think she had a chance," Sorcha said.

"Hey! Not nice. Finn's a decent guy. He wouldn't do that to anyone," Vorana said.

Sorcha shrugged. "It was probably about a woman then. Maybe they're both interested in the same girl, and it's causing friction in their friendship."

"There's no one new in Crimson Cove for them to fight over," Vorana said. "And Finn can never keep quiet when he's got his eye on someone. He hasn't talked about anyone special recently."

"There you have it! He's sneaking around with someone Torrin is interested in because he knows what will happen when he figures it out." Sorcha stabbed her food with a fork. "They always have to be messing around, mistreating the people they're supposed to care about. We all know how complicated relationships are."

"Not all relationships are complicated." Vorana exchanged a discreet glance of concern with Zandra.

"Point out one relationship that isn't on its last legs, or the couple isn't hiding secrets from each other. That's trouble." Sorcha waved her fork in the air.

Vorana gently set down her knife. "Don't become a man-hater. You got unlucky with Gaian, but there are decent guys out there."

"None of them are coming my way," Sorcha grumbled. "Not that I want them. I'm seriously considering banning all males from entering my café."

Sorcha was still suffering following her humiliating mistreatment by Gaian Scythe. We'd all been fooled by him at first, although his true colors had seeped out now and again, so I'd always had my suspicions. He'd used powerful magic on Sorcha to bend her to his will. It was no wonder her heart felt bruised. She'd been in love, and he'd used her fondness as a weapon in his magical war chest to attempt to take over the town.

Sorcha opened her mouth, most likely to keep ranting about how awful the male of the species was, but I beat her to it. "I should warn you all. Ember Dreamscape is back in town."

"What's that little snitch doing here?" Sage said. "And why haven't the angels thrown him in prison yet and lost the magical key so he never gets out?"

"There's been a change of plans. Ember has turned against the gremlins and will testify against everyone involved in the attack on Crimson Cove."

"You mean he'll get away with what he did to us?" Sage stamped a paw. "That's unacceptable."

"He's not in the clear," I said. "He's going through the same intensive rehab as Sammy and Tinkerbell. And he'll receive some sort of sentence, although I'm unsure what that'll be. Angel Force is still figuring things out. Barney has taken an interest in Sammy's rehabilitation, though, so there's a chance you'll see Ember walking around Crimson Cove."

"I'm making a complaint," Sage said. "Angel Force has been too soft on Ember. They took one look at that irritating, fluffy face and assumed he could do no wrong. But we were all at the Whispering Willow Inn. Ember could have killed us. He still might if Barney falls under his devious charms."

"Ember sounds almost as bad as Gaian." Sorcha wrinkled her nose when she said his name, as if she smelled something rotten.

"We'll keep an eye on Ember," Zandra said. "At the first sign of trouble, we'll let the angels know."

"I'm still not happy," Sage said. "Trouble follows that young cat. Don't let Barney get taken in by his innocent charm, or he'll be the next magic user manipulated into performing dark deeds for that fluffy menace."

"Sage, Ember is a young cat. He made a mistake," Vorana said.

"He could have killed you!"

"You'd never have let him. You watch me like a hawk, and I'm grateful for it." Vorana reached over and tickled Sage under the chin. "Eat up before your food gets cold. Are the pieces cut small enough?"

"They're fine. Don't baby me." Sage hoovered up a third of the meat on her plate and slurped it down in noisy bites. She was stress eating.

"Barney knows what's going on," I said. "He's being cautious with Ember and using magical restraints whenever he takes him out of his pen."

Sage grumbled and groused some more while we ate dinner.

"Has Finn said anything about dragons to you?" Vorana said.

Zandra raised her eyebrows and glanced at me. "What makes you ask?"

"He's been coming into the store and ordering books on dragon care. I joked with him that he must be considering adoption, and he went pale and hurried out. He didn't even take his book with him."

"Of course! That's why Torrin came to the sanctuary," I said.

"Juno! We don't know for certain why Torrin was there." Zandra's face expressed caution.

"Do you know something?" Vorana said.

"We can trust them. We're all friends," I said. "Finn won't mind us sharing his news. But it must go no further than these four walls."

"He's dating multiple girls in secret, isn't he?" Sorcha said. "How many have found out and are after him?"

"It's not that." I paused. Should Finn's dragon issue stay hidden? If Vorana and Sorcha knew, they could help. "It has to do with Vorana's adoption theory."

"I knew it! Finn ordered half a dozen books and spent an hour browsing the dragon shelves in the store," Vorana said. "I know he occasionally helps injured dragons when there's nowhere else for them to go, but these books were on hatchling care. What's he up to? I was joking when I mentioned adoption, but now I'm not so sure. Does he want a hatchling to care for?"

"He's lost his mind if he's thinking about adopting a baby dragon," Sorcha said.

"Finn's a half-demon. He'd be strong enough to control one. At least a baby." Vorana leaned in close, her eyes shining. "Go on, Juno. You know we'll find out soon, anyway. Especially if Finn starts carrying a scaled baby around in a papoose."

I stared at Zandra until she sighed and nodded. "Tell them. But if Finn gets angry because we couldn't stay quiet about his secret, this is on you."

Everyone waited, looking at me to share the scaly secret.

"Finn's got himself into trouble," I said. "Some time ago, a dragon egg was left at the sanctuary gate."

"I remember that happening," Vorana said. "No one could figure out why it got left. Dragons take great care of their infants, and they'd never willingly abandon an egg."

"We assumed someone stole it from a dragon but then realized how hot the property was. They didn't want the baby to die, but they didn't dare risk taking the egg back to where they'd stolen it from, so they left it with Finn, knowing it would be looked after," I said.

"And he meant to find the egg a proper home," Zandra said.

Vorana tilted her head. "But there was a problem?"

"The baby sang to Finn," Zandra said. "He's bonded with her."

Vorana gasped. "No wonder he's been so worried. Dragon mama will want that egg back."

"She can have it," Sorcha said. "We don't want dragons rampaging around Crimson Cove and burning it to a crisp while they fight over the baby. Finn has to give it back."

"He's not sure he can," I said. "A bond with an infant dragon runs deep. And, of course, the baby sensed Finn's qualities and knew she'd have a safe haven with him. Why wouldn't she want to bond with him?"

"It isn't the baby dragon's fault," Zandra said. "She wants a parent to care for her."

"I never said it was. It's Finn's fault," Sorcha said. "Of course, typical guy, not thinking logically and doing exactly what he wants. He probably thinks it's cool to own a dragon."

I chose not to pick apart Sorcha's illogical argument. "You're right about Finn being nervous. He said he felt like he was being watched when we were at the bakery opening. I've also noticed a pungent sulfurous smell around the sanctuary. And I saw something large lurking in the shadows."

"And that thunder we heard," Zandra said. "That was dragon noise, wasn't it? They're on to Finn."

I nodded. "I believe so."

"Where has he got the egg hidden?" Vorana asked.

"At the sanctuary," I said. "That was why Torrin showed up. He's a half-dragon. He must be acting as a go-between to see if they can negotiate with the dragons."

"With his temper?" Vorana shook her head. "Torrin inherited the same hot-headedness as any dragon I've ever met but half the tact. If he says the wrong thing to the wrong dragon, this situation could get fiery fast."

"This is bad," Sorcha said. "I've seen Torrin at his worst, and it's not pretty. Things get burned."

Vorana pushed back her seat. "We need to intervene. Get Finn to see sense. And if Torrin is acting as the go-between, we must ensure he doesn't put his foot in it and start a dragon war."

Zandra moved her food around her plate with her fork. "Normally, I'd be right there with you, but we've got too much going on to deal with dragons."

"We have?" I asked.

"Work's busy. We have Hortense's murder to focus on. You want me to date Randal. And now dragons! There's only so much one person can handle."

"But you're more than one person," I said. "You have me. I'm equal to at least a dozen very capable persons."

Zandra's expression turned acerbic. "You know what I mean. If I juggle too much, something will break. I don't want that thing to be me. Or you. Or Randal. And I'm not letting Barney down."

"I didn't know you were dating Randal again," Vorana said. "I saw you together at the bakery reopening. It's finally happening?"

"Yes," I said at the same time as Zandra said, "No."

She sighed. "I'm exploring possibilities. But that's it. As I said, there's a lot going on. I short-changed Randal the last time we attempted dating, and I won't do it again."

"You can always make time to date. And Randal is adorable," I said.

"Dating's for idiots," Sorcha said. "You should follow my lead and commit to the single life. It's the only time I'm truly happy."

She looked the opposite of happy as she stabbed her food and scowled.

While the group discussed Randal's merits and whether dating was for idiots, I leaned closer to Sage, who had a full mouth of dinner and was chomping noisily. "I need your help."

She glanced at me out of the corner of her eye and kept chomping.

"We need to go on a kitten impossible mission. You in?"

She grunted.

"This is important. We need to keep our magic users safe from dragons."

Sage paused her chomping. She looked at Vorana then nodded.

"Good. When everyone's gone to sleep tonight, we're going hunting."

Chapter 9

Cashed in

It had just passed midnight, and I was hurrying along the silent streets of Crimson Cove with Sage by my side, the faint squeak of her harness wheel the only noise disturbing the night.

"Are we hunting dragons or planning on doing something with the egg?" Sage asked.

"We'll look for any signs dragons have been at the sanctuary," I said, "but we have to get that egg out of there. The baby is hatching soon, and once she enters the world, the other dragons will find her. You can't keep hatchlings silent. If she sends out alarm cries, angry dragons will engulf the sanctuary, and they'll take no prisoners when they reclaim their baby."

Sage huffed out her agreement. "What was Finn thinking, getting himself messed up in this?"

"He got distracted. His life has been busy. I don't think he meant to keep the egg, but once a baby dragon attaches to you, you're in trouble."

Sage walked in silence for a moment. "He'll make a good father."

"He'll be a dead one if we don't fix this problem. Let's hurry. I know where the egg is. The shed is surrounded by magic, but we can break through. We'll transport the egg back to Vorana's, and—"

"No! Not there. I don't want dragons skulking around the house. We'll take the egg to the storage facility where Vorana keeps her excess stock. It's secure and quiet. No one will bother us, and the dragons will never know the egg is stashed there."

"Fair enough. I don't want my witch exposed to dragons, either."

We arrived at the sanctuary. Two rooms were lit up in the converted barn where the volunteers stayed, but other than the occasional soft grunt or hoof stamp from residents, the place was quiet.

I led Sage to the shed where the egg was stored. "The magic barrier is down. Maybe Finn forgot to put it up the last time he checked on the egg."

Sage was glaring into the shadows. "Let's hurry. Get in there and move the egg."

I dashed to the door, tugged down the handle with my paws, and it swung open. I ran to the pile of straw. The egg was gone.

"Where is it?" Sage asked. "You said it was in here."

I hissed softly. "Finn must have moved it. He must be feeling jittery if he thinks this location is no longer secure from snooping dragons."

"You think the egg is in another barn?"

"Perhaps he's put it in with some of the other animals in the hope they'd mask the smell."

We headed back to the barns where the sanctuary residents stayed. We checked the storage barns first, but there was no sign of the egg. Then we went into the small animal enclosure. There was a mixture of critters, from tiny musk rats with wings to robust cat familiars that had gone astray or been injured.

We checked a few pens, apologizing to any residents we disturbed.

"Hey, what are you doing?" a sharp, quiet voice said from the darkness of one pen.

"Greetings!" I whispered. "Sorry for disturbing your sleep, but we're looking for something."

"You'll only find trouble if you keep poking around. Get out of here. You and your clumpy-footed buddy are messing with my snoozing time."

"I have a question then I'll leave you alone," I said.

There was silence. Then a sigh. "I'm awake now. What is it?"

"Has Finn been in and left anything new in this barn?"

"Like what? People are always coming in and out."

"It could have a slightly sulfurous scent. It may have happened yesterday evening or earlier today. Were you here?"

There was a shuffling in the darkness, and a small brown lizard-like creature with stunted wings and a long tail slid toward us. He had a glowing cast on one leg. "Do you mean a dragon?"

"I didn't explicitly say dragon," I said. "But I see you're familiar with that species and their curious scent. May I ask what you are?" Although the creature's skin was brown, he wasn't a dull brown but a mottled, scaled bronze. Really beautiful. And as he extended his wings, they were larger than I'd thought. It was possible he had the ability to fly if his bones were light.

"I'm a hybrid. Kind of dragon-like. More like a wyvern but also not. And not good enough to be accepted by either," he said.

"Are you rare?"

"Yeah. And not popular. Most people think we're worthless."

"Is that how you came to be here? Someone gave you up?"

"I got lost and injured. My owner will come for me, though." He puffed out his chest, and a small red leathery ruff lifted around his neck. "Bell doesn't know I'm in trouble yet. If she did, she'd be here. I told her I'd be out all night so she won't know I'm missing until the morning."

"How did you get injured?"

"Stop gas bagging. We don't have time," Sage whispered. "Does he know anything about the you-know-what or not?"

"Of course. Did Finn bring anything dragon-related in here?" I asked.

The wyvern creature shook his head. "I'd know if there was anything like that here. There has been something with a dragon smell hanging around, though. When I was outside getting exercise, I saw shadows. Dragons are incredible at disguising themselves in the clouds, so they can do flybys and nobody sees what they're up to. But I've been around them most of my life, so I know what to watch out for."

"That proves dragons are interested in Finn," I said to Sage. "Do you know what their intentions are?"

"The fact they're watching and not making any moves suggests they're gathering data. What's Finn gotten himself into that the dragons want a piece of him?" the wyvern creature asked.

"That's what we're helping him with," I said. "Thank you. Sorry, I didn't get your name."

"Barnabas Hodgepodge the Third. Bonded to Bell Blackthorn. Servant to the Ithric Dynasty." He swooped his chest low to the ground and extended his wings.

"It's been a pleasure, Barnabas. I hope you make a speedy recovery. You'll get the best care here. As soon as you're able, Finn will be happy to send you home to Bell."

"He won't if he gets his head chewed off by an angry dragon," Sage muttered.

We looked around the rest of the barns but found no sign of the egg.

"What about this place?" Sage walked toward the barn with the lights on.

"This is the volunteer quarters," I said. "I'm surprised anyone's awake, though. Maybe an animal needed caring for. There could be babies that need feeding."

"Or they left the lights on for security. We should take a look."

Since we'd looked everywhere else, I had no problem trying one final place. We entered cautiously, but there was no sign of anyone at home. There was a compact kitchen and dining area, a small sitting room, and up a flight of stairs, three bedrooms. None of them were currently occupied, although they all looked like they'd recently been used.

I sniffed the air as we entered the room with the light on. "This place smells like Dawn." A quick look around the room revealed familiar items of clothing that I'd seen her wearing.

"Let's make this speedy," Sage said. "I don't want her catching us if she's only in the bathroom."

There weren't many places to look. A small closet, under the bed, and a chest of drawers.

"What's this?" Sage tugged out a large bulging backpack. "You could fit an egg in here if you were careful."

"Does it feel egg-like?" I hurried over and sniffed the backpack. "I don't get a hint of sulfur."

"It's too soft. Probably clothes that need to go in the wash."

I tugged open the drawstring and tipped the backpack on its side. Clothes tumbled out, but wrapped inside them was a bundle of money. And we weren't talking a small amount. There was probably a few thousand in there.

I sat back and inspected the unexpected find. "Dawn volunteers here, so she doesn't get paid, and from what Finn told us, she hasn't been successful in holding down a job."

"Maybe it has something to do with this." Sage nudged a small black notebook toward me with her nose. "There are sums of money written in it. Maybe she's collecting it."

"Collections for what?" I flipped through the pages. There were neat initials, and beside each one, a sum of money. Some of them were large.

"Hey! What are you doing?" Dawn dashed into the room, a mug in one hand. She grabbed the money and the notebook and held them against her chest as she backed away, rage firing bright dots of color on each cheek.

"Greetings, Dawn. We're investigating a crime for Angel Force," I said. "I didn't think you were home."

"Clearly not, since you're going through my stuff without my permission." She looked down at the money. "You gonna steal this?"

"No! But we're curious as to how it came into your possession. Did you earn it?"

Her nostrils flared. "That's none of your business."

"It is if it has anything to do with what happened to Hortense."

"What? Hortense? You think this is payment for killing her? I'm a hit woman?" Her laughter grated out of her, harsh and high in pitch.

"Did Hortense give you that money?" I asked.

"This has nothing to do with her. Go hassle someone else." Dawn tucked the money under one armpit.

"Savings from a job?"

She pressed her lips together. "It's my money. It doesn't matter how I got it. I can get you in trouble for this. I don't see a search warrant from Angel Force authorizing this search, so I'll tell them I caught you robbing me."

"As freelance consultants, we—"

"I don't believe you. You claim to work for Angel Force, but they'd never do anything like this. I've been around the angels plenty of times, and they do things by the book. If this was an official search, there'd be angels here and paperwork."

"They've searched your home before?" Sage asked. "Why would that be?"

Dawn glowered at Sage. "If you were involved with Angel Force, you'd be able to access that information. Now, both of you, get out of here unless you want real trouble."

I stood my ground. "We want no trouble, but we do want to find out what happened to Hortense."

"Then look elsewhere! You won't get a confession out of me."

I stared at the money partially concealed under Dawn's arm. Was the cash connected to Hortense's murder? Dawn didn't work, so if someone offered her a large sum to get rid of a Hortense-shaped problem, she may have been tempted.

"Stop it! I know what you're thinking. I've already told you my alibi, and that's all you need to know. Nothing else matters." Dawn set down her mug then grabbed the backpack and stuffed the money and the notebook back inside. "If you want someone to go after, someone who had a reason to kill Hortense, speak to pesky Percival. Ask him why he's still lurking around."

"The camera operator?" I asked. "What do you know about him?"

"Hortense had a blowup with him. She didn't know anyone was watching when they fought." Dawn stuffed the backpack between the closet and the chest of drawers. She stood in front of it, her arms folded. "I heard raised voices, went to take a peek, and Hortense was jabbing a finger in Percival's face and yelling at him. She said he was disrespectful and had no right to film her."

"Hortense didn't want to be on camera?"

"I reckon she didn't. Percival protested, said he was just doing his job, and since Hortense seemed to be in charge, he wanted to get footage of her."

"She didn't take kindly to that?"

"It made her angrier. She grabbed the camera off his shoulder and threw it to the ground. Then Percival got angry. Like really mean. He yelled and tried to grab her, but she shoved him away. He shoved back. Hard. He's not a nice guy."

"How did Hortense react?" I asked.

"She didn't back down. She tried to stamp on the camera, but Percival grabbed it and called her crazy. Then he left." Dawn remained in front of the backpack.

"He shouldn't have shoved Hortense, but he had a right to be angry," Sage said. "Sounds like Hortense had her own anger issues to deal with."

Dawn shrugged. "Percival was a jerk to all of us. I made the mistake of asking him what he was doing, and he called me an idiot and said I got in the way of the perfect shot, and he'd have to redo it because my irritating voice was on the footage. I didn't know he was doing anything special!"

I was still suspicious of Dawn and her hidden bundle of money and the notebook with the odd initials inside, but this new information about Percival could be relevant.

Dawn continued, "I'm guessing Percival was angry because Hortense damaged his equipment. And she made him look like a fool, so he saw an opportunity for payback and took it. He was wandering around the sanctuary the evening she was killed, taking pictures and filming us. Maybe he saw Hortense go into that barn and followed her. They could have argued again. And why is he still in town? He's got his footage. He's staying to listen to gossip and see if anyone is pointing the finger at him. And if they aren't, they should be."

I looked at the backpack, and Dawn moved to block my view. "I appreciate the information. And sorry for searching your room without your permission. We meant no harm. We do want to get to the bottom of what happened to Hortense."

Dawn scowled but then raised her shoulders. "I get it. Don't do it again. And keep your paws out of my stuff. I've not got much, but what I have, I'm not giving up without a fight."

We hurried out of the room and left the barn.

"You think Dawn was hiding something?" Sage said.

"That money and the notepad are suspicious, and maybe she used the information about Percival as a diversion. I've yet to double-check Dawn's alibi, but she's given us a solid lead on another suspect."

"So, we came here for a dragon egg and got a murder suspect. Not a wasted evening."

I slowed and tilted my head. "Did you hear that?"

"That was my stomach. I'm late for my usual midnight snack."

I took a step toward a dark clump of bushes. "There it is again."

"That wasn't my stomach. Some sort of rat? I could catch it for Vorana. Leave it in her purse. She'd love that."

I crept past the bushes into the dense, chilly gloom. If it wasn't for my incredible cat eyesight, I wouldn't be able to see a thing, but I'd picked out the outline of a small box tucked behind a tree.

"Don't look for trouble, Juno. We've got enough to deal with," Sage whispered.

I ignored her as I cautiously crept closer to the chirruping box. There was a sting of magic around it that had me recoiling, but after a few swipes of my paw, I disabled the spell.

"Don't do it," Sage said.

I couldn't resist and eased off the box lid. My breath escaped me as I stared down at a tiny sparkling white dragon hatchling.

She looked up at me, blinked once, and then said, "Mama?"

Chapter 10

Scaled dilemma

"You can't bring that thing back to Vorana's!" Sage stomped along beside me, her harness rattling and her breath rasping out in angry pants.

"It's not a thing. It's an adorable female dragon hatchling. And she's clinging to my neck so tightly, I can barely breathe." The second the baby called me mama, I knew I was in trouble. She'd launched herself at me and refused to let go. Currently, she had one of my ears in her mouth and was sucking on it.

"Even though that's a baby dragon, it's still a dragon. Once she gets the hang of how to light her flame, she'll burn the house down. Infants have no control over their emotions or behavior, no matter what kind of magical creature they are. Which is why she shouldn't be with us."

"What were we supposed to do? Leave her in the woods? She's vulnerable."

"She's a freakin' dragon!"

"She's a newborn infant with no idea how to look after herself," I said. "For now, she stays with us."

"Not at Vorana's house. I won't put my witch in harm's way."

"Vorana will help to ensure we can control this baby. She has books on every subject. And I don't know the first thing about looking after a dragon hatchling."

Sage grumbled and groused. "Another reason I'm right and you're wrong."

I stopped walking and turned to her. "Tell me where to dump her, then. Will the middle of the road be suitable? Then she'll be crushed quickly. Or how about the nearest trash container? Isn't it a recycling day? She'll soon be squished into a tiny blob of scaly nothingness."

Sage glared at me then her gaze flicked to the infant. "I don't want her dead."

"That's what'll happen if we abandon her."

Sage snorted. "Let's keep going. I'll go inside, but you wait outside with the baby. And stay away from anything flammable."

"She's hungry. I can't feed her grass. And this is one heavy baby I've got latched to my throat. We need a pit stop and a refuel. When we get inside, I'll open the back door and direct her mouth outward in case any unexpected flames emerge. But we have nothing to worry about. She won't breathe fire on her first day of life."

"Says you, who knows nothing about baby dragons." Sage hissed at me. "If this goes wrong, I'm blaming you. And I'll never talk to you again if anything bad happens to Vorana."

"Don't you think she's even the tiniest bit adorable?" I attempted to drag my ear from the dragon's mouth, but she whimpered, so I gave up the fight.

"If you like scales and sparkles."

"I do. And so do you. She's young and needs help. Our help. How can you refuse her?"

"She needs to be with a dragon who can look after her properly," Sage said. "But now she's attached herself to you and Finn, it's complicated things. Nothing is ever simple with you."

The dragon let go of my ear and coughed out acrid smoke that made us gag.

Sage scurried away. "You see! She's about to launch her first flame."

"Then we should hurry. But you're overreacting. They take weeks to find their fiery voice."

"This one's the exception. I know what'll happen. She'll set the house on fire, injure my witch, and then a horde of angry dragons will descend from the sky and destroy us."

"I love how you see the bright side of every challenge. Let's get the baby fed, figure out how to look after her, and then we'll make our next move."

"If we're even alive to make a move."

Sage grumbled all the way to the house. The baby was content to keep sucking my ear, and I kept a watchful eye out for marauding dragons who may have picked up her scent. So far, we'd been lucky, and I felt no threat in the shadows.

We reached the house, crept inside, and snuck into the kitchen. Sage used magic to unlock the back door and insisted I sit beside it with the baby's head facing outside.

The dragon lifted her nose and sniffed the air. She smacked her beaky lips together.

"I told you she was hungry," I said.

"Vorana doesn't have any maidens tied to a stake in the fridge. Or armored knights on quests defrosting on the counter," Sage said.

"That's the stuff of fairy tales. Some kind of pureed meat should work. Maybe some of that finest quality raw food Vorana tried you on. You don't like it."

"It's bland. There's some in the fridge. Keep that baby by the door. I'll go get it."

"Some for me, too."

Sage stomped to the fridge, floated up on a spell, pulled open the door, and grabbed a white bowl. She floated back down to the floor and shoved it toward us with her head.

I gently encouraged the hatchling to sniff the food. It took a few minutes, but she detached her mouth from my ear and attempted to eat. It was messy and ineffective, but some of the food went down the right way, although most of it got smeared across her face, which I licked off, much to her delight.

I sampled the raw food too, which was indeed bland, while Sage munched down big mouthfuls of dried kibble, not taking her eyes off of the hungry dragon.

"Don't look at her like that. It's not her fault she ended up at Finn's sanctuary." I carefully moved the bowl, so the dragon stopped trying to eat a floor tile.

"I still can't believe he did this. That angel must be out of his mind for thinking he could keep a hatchling a secret."

"Finn's under the influence of her thrall song," I said. "But it's a good thing she's on our side. Weird things happen in Crimson Cove, and having a dragon friend will be a bonus."

"Only if she doesn't turn on us and bite our heads off."

The baby chirped happily, having finally gotten the hang of how to feed herself. Her stomach slowly plumped up and her scales glowed.

I smiled. "She's too adorable to even think about biting our heads off."

"We should return her to the dragons," Sage said. "If we tell them it was a mistake and the idiot who kept the egg didn't know what he was doing, they may forgive Finn, and us, for getting involved when we shouldn't."

"Dragons aren't a forgiving bunch," I said. "And they're traditional. They have hundreds of protocols and rules that must be followed."

Sage snorted a laugh. "Maybe they'll force you to marry Finn. The baby thinks you're its mother, and Finn is the father. That would make a pairing."

"Finn would be thrilled to be married to me. I'd make anyone a charming partner."

"Charming is not the word I'd use. Not at this moment." Sage finished the last mouthful of kibble and stared hard at the baby. "I guess she is cute. Do all hatchlings glow?"

"I have no clue. Which is why we need help. It's time you woke Vorana."

"What about Zandra? If I'm putting my witch at risk, you must involve Zandra, too."

"I'll introduce her to the dragon. But the sooner we find out everything we need about caring for this infant, the better. I don't know if she's had enough to eat or how much she drinks or how warm we need to keep her."

Sage sighed. "I'll go get Vorana before you and your daughter burn this place to the ground."

"There's no need." Vorana's sleepy voice drifted along the hallway. "What are you two up to?"

Neither of us spoke as Vorana entered the kitchen. Her sleepy gaze sharpened when she saw the hatchling. "Oh! What have you got there?"

"A fiery problem wrapped in scales," Sage said. "This is Juno's fault. And Finn's. I blame them equally."

"This is Finn's dragon?" Vorana inched closer then crouched. "How adorable. Hey, baby. Welcome to the world."

"I knew she'd like her," I said to Sage.

Vorana reached for the hatchling, but the infant hissed, and smoke blasted from her mouth. Then she flared her tiny, sticky wings and growled.

Sage darted forward and boxed the baby dragon around the head. "Don't even think about attacking my magic user. She's in charge around here. This is her home, so respect her."

The hatchling scurried back and bumped into me. She scrambled onto my back and bit my ear.

"Don't scare her," I said.

"She made an aggressive move toward Vorana. And if you don't reprimand them when they're young, they never know right from wrong." Sage bared her yellowed teeth at the dragon. "Stay away from my witch."

"It's okay." Vorana stroked Sage until her hackles flattened. "I startled her. She's so beautiful. But where is Finn? Why isn't he looking after her?"

"The idiot moved the egg. The baby hatched and was all alone. We found her," Sage said. "Juno had the dumb idea to bring her here, and nothing I said would change her mind."

Vorana kept her attention fixed on the hatchling. "What were you doing out at this time of night?"

"We were on one of Juno's harebrained missions. It didn't involve a baby dragon, though, but we got sidetracked."

"This baby is a welcome diversion," I said. "And I'm glad we found her. She must have been scared when she cracked open her egg and she was alone."

"We must handle her carefully," Vorana said. "Hatchlings are vulnerable. They have trouble regulating their body temperature."

"Which is why we came here," I said. "We need to know everything about keeping this baby alive."

"She's not staying," Sage said. "I want her out by sun up."

"Sage! We can't throw the hatchling out on her own." Vorana shook her head.

"Then we'll toss Juno out with her since she landed us in this mess."

"Oh, hush. And stop grousing. You're only grumpy because you're tired. Go take a nap, and we'll research what to do with the hatchling. It looks like you're on the right track, though. She's feeding okay?" Vorana asked me.

"She likes Sage's raw meat," I said.

"I'll get more out of the freezer. Then I'll grab a book on dragon care."

"I'm not sleeping. I'll guard the dragon," Sage said. "Is she looking at me funny?"

I shuffled the hatchling into a comfy position on my back. "No! I'm taking her to meet Zandra."

"If you see so much as a flicker of flame from that dragon's mouth, bring her here and we'll sit her in a bowl of water." Sage hissed at the hatchling.

"I'll do no such thing! She'll get cold."

Sage followed us to the top of the basement stairs then sat guard, glaring at us as we made our way down.

Zandra was still asleep, and with the dragon on my back, I was unable to jump onto the bed, so I put my meowing technique to good use. Several howls later, Zandra stirred.

"You'd better have the worst stomach ache in the world if you're making that kind of noise," she muttered. "Where are you?"

"Down here," I said. "And I have a surprise."

There was silence for a few seconds. "Is it a dead surprise?"

"This surprise is very much alive. Look! You'll love it."

The hatchling had stilled at the sound of Zandra's voice, but she still sucked on my ear.

Zandra's head appeared over the side of the bed. She blinked several times, as if not believing what she was seeing. "How did you get that?"

"This is Finn's baby dragon. Sort of mine now, too." I explained my visit to Finn's sanctuary, what we'd found in Dawn's room, and how I came to have a dragon attached to me, chewing on my ear.

"Huh! Well, it's better than a dead rat or a rotting squirrel pelt."

"That squirrel pelt was perfectly serviceable."

"If you have no sense of smell." Zandra slid gently out of bed. "Although this surprise has the potential to be deadlier than a moldy pelt."

"I couldn't leave her!"

Zandra lifted a hand to quell my protest. "I'd have done the same. And she's taken to you. Well, she likes your ear."

"Sucking is a source of comfort for newborns," I said. "Although I'll have to get her to swap ears soon. The one in her mouth is numb, and I can already feel her teeth."

"Do I smell burning?" Sage shouted down the stairs.

"No! We're fine," I said. "Sage doesn't trust the baby not to blow us up with a fiery burp."

"No surprise there. You have a miniature killing machine on your back, so we need to watch her."

"You don't like her?"

"I didn't say that." Zandra tilted her head as she inspected the infant. "She's pretty. But I'm not forgetting that dragons are apex predators. And this one's family will be looking for her."

"We'll figure that out," I said.

Zandra stood and stretched. "How? We need a plan."

"I've worked one out. First, strong coffee for you and Vorana while you look over the best way to keep the hatchling alive."

"Sounds good so far. What else?"

"Then we talk to Finn about his newborn."

"If he's bonded with her, he won't give her up easily," Zandra said.

"We'll convince him it's the right thing to do. Finn's life is at risk if he doesn't return what isn't his."

"So is ours if the dragons think we kidnapped their baby and plan to raise her as our own. Anything else to put on the things-to-do-so-we-don't-die list?"

"We must speak to Percival, the camera guy who was filming at the sanctuary."

"After what you've told me about him, that makes sense. And we need to figure out how Dawn got so rich without having a job," Zandra said.

"She wasn't happy we found her money," I said. "I suspect it was obtained illegally."

"Which makes her our prime suspect in Hortense's murder?"

"She has an alibi, but it's worth double-checking for holes. She could have stolen the money from Hortense or been given it to kill her."

Zandra looked longingly at her bed. "Let's get to work. No more sleep for us while we have a newborn in the house and a murder to solve."

Chapter 11

Family ties

We spent hours researching the best way to take care of a dragon hatchling. Vorana was a wonderful source of information, even finding original texts written by a dragon on how to care for their infants. We soon had a routine in place for the baby, including a feeding schedule, naptime, and bathing. Sage was still furious the hatchling was staying at Vorana's, but we decided she needed to stay with us until we'd spoken to Finn and made sure he had a plan in place that wouldn't get him killed.

Which was how I came to be hiding in the alleyway behind Vorana's bookstore with the dragon still attached to me, while Zandra went to Angel Force to update Finn that he was now a father.

It was risky being outside with the hatchling, but she wouldn't let go of me, and if the dragons were watching Finn, we didn't want to lead them to Vorana's house. Sage was adamant about that and had hissed at me until I'd agreed to take the baby with me.

It was still early, and the only passing traffic was people hurrying to open their stores. I was glad of the quiet since the infant was lively and chirped every time she saw someone.

"You must be on your best behavior," I whispered. "You're about to meet your father. Well, your angel father. Half-angel, half-demon father. Families are so complicated. But you picked well by forming an alliance with Finn. He protects his friends, and I know he'll protect you."

The baby chirped happily. I'd persuaded her my other ear was as tasty as the original ear she'd latched onto, and in between throaty chirrups, she kept sucking on it. I could tell she'd grown since I last picked her up. It wouldn't be long before she was too heavy to carry. Then we'd have a problem on our paws.

Binky and Tia walked past the entrance to the alleyway. Binky turned her head and lifted her large nose, inhaling deeply. She locked eyes with me, and her gaze widened.

I shook my head and shooed her away with one paw. She took the hint and carried on with Tia, but I knew she'd be back. And it was sooner than I'd expected, the ground shaking beneath my paws, announcing her return.

"Did anyone see you come this way?" I whispered as Binky approached, her stunned gaze on the infant.

"I don't think so. What you got there? I knew I smelled something odd. Is that a—"

"Go check and make sure no one saw you. Quick!"

Binky hesitated, torn between sniffing the hatchling and following my order, then turned and hurried back to the entrance of the alleyway. She looked around then returned. "It's all clear. Juno! What are you doing with a baby dragon on your back? Is it real?"

"Hush! You didn't see us. This is a covert operation of the highest importance."

She went to sniff the hatchling but got growled at, and smoke swirled around us, making Binky step back and cough. "She's feisty for something so small. Stinks, too."

"Don't forget it. And don't be rude about her smell. She's yet to have her first bath."

Binky's large furry nose wrinkled. "You're adopting her?"

"She adopted me. Let's call it fostering. Short-term fostering while we figure out what to do with her. How's Tia?"

"Oh! Good. Better now I've been released." Binky attempted to sniff the hatchling again, but a plume of acrid smoke from the baby's mouth convinced her it was a bad idea. "I still can't believe Cythera locked me up for protecting Tia. What did she expect me to do when she came after her so aggressively?"

"Cythera was aggressive? I've seen her surly and abrupt with suspects, but she never uses unnecessary force."

"She was flaring her wings, and we all know what that means. When I gave her a warning nip—"

"Apologies for interrupting, but you bit Cythera?"

"Not a full bite. I didn't use all my teeth. She was stressing Tia, so I had to make her back off. I growled, hissed, stalked around her several times, but she wouldn't take the hint. Then this jumped-up new angel got involved. That's when I turned up the meanometer."

I chuckled. "Takes pluck to bite a member of Angel Force."

"She'll think twice before going after Tia again." Binky raised a velveteen paw and touched the hatchling. "Are you any closer to finding out what happened to Hortense? Tia's still nervous about Angel Force coming back for a second round of questioning."

"We have leads. We got distracted, though, by this." I lifted my head and bumped the back of it against the baby.

"No surprise. She sure is cute. You should keep her. She likes you."

"Our home isn't dragon-proof. And Sage is making a stink about keeping a fire-breathing creature so close to Vorana."

"I see why that would be a problem. I'd be just as protective of Tia." Binky settled on the ground, content to stay with us. "I've been thinking about the murder. Have you heard of a volunteer at the sanctuary called Augustus?"

"I have. You know something about him?"

"I've been helping at the sanctuary while the bakery was remodeled. I was getting under Tia's feet and didn't want to annoy her, so I'd wander over there. I like helping." Binky's furred nose wrinkled. "I didn't take to Augustus when he showed up. He acts like a decent guy, but it's a front."

"You've seen him misbehave?" I adjusted the hatchling's weight, so she wasn't pressing so hard on my head.

"He gossips about everyone. And it's not nice gossip. He's mean about people but then fakes being nice to their face. I've heard him say something mean about everyone. Even Finn. Then he was all big smiles and clapping Finn on the back the next time he saw him. That's double standards. Untrustworthy."

"We've yet to speak to Augustus, but he's another suspect's alibi, so if they were together, then it can't have been him," I said. "I didn't realize he had a devious nature, though."

"He called me an overgrown tabby when he thought I wasn't around." Binky whined. "It hurt my feelings. And he always has food in his beard. I don't get big beards. It's like long-haired animals. They must spend most of their time grooming to get food or old twigs out of their undercoat. If I had a long coat, I'd shave it. It's kind of gross."

"Did you ever overhear Augustus say bad things about Hortense?" I asked.

"All the time! But when he was hanging out with her, he'd say mean things about other people. I think he does it to get everyone to like him."

"Did Hortense ever hear Augustus make mean comments about her?"

Binky chuffed out a laugh. "She caught him mid-gossip! She was always sticking her nose into other people's business. One day, they got into a fight about it. I missed the beginning of the argument, but Augustus walked off and said she'd regret making fun of him. He said he had power, and he wasn't afraid to use it."

"Does he have significant magic? I sensed nothing uniquely magical about him."

"He's your average warlock. But Hortense could have made him mad, so he got his revenge when no one was watching. Augustus is sneaky. Don't trust him."

Finn appeared at the end of the alleyway. His expression brightened as he saw the hatchling on my back. He hurried toward us, Zandra behind him.

"I should go," Binky said. "Tia will wonder where I am. I said I'd only be five minutes."

"Thanks for the information about Augustus," I said.

"No problem. Happy to help." Binky tried to lick the hatchling but dashed away when she huffed pungent smoke into her face.

"Wow! She's so beautiful." Finn dropped to his knees in front of me and the hatchling, awe on his face. "How did I get so lucky?"

The hatchling stared at Finn. Her body tensed then she jumped off me and into Finn's arms. He embraced her and held her against his chest, crooning softly to her. The hatchling chirped and purred, squirming in his arms, her small tail wrapped tightly around one of Finn's wrists.

"This looks like a happy family reunion," Zandra said, an amused look on her face.

"I thought you were joking when you told me she'd hatched." Finn couldn't take his eyes off the baby. "But here she is!"

"Why did you leave her alone in the woods?" I asked sharply. "The egg was active when you showed it to us."

"I was convinced she wouldn't hatch for at least another week. The egg had gone silent again, so I figured she'd gone back into hibernation because she knew it was a bad time to come out."

"Why move her at all?"

Finn winced. "I got paranoid after showing you the shed. Then Cythera almost caught me. I had to do something."

"So you left her alone in the woods! Anything could have gotten her."

Finn dropped his head. "Sorry, baby. You should have let me know you had plans to come out sooner than expected. I'd have waited with you. You weren't scared, were you?"

The hatchling didn't seem to mind and was content to nuzzle Finn, ignoring me. I tried not to feel slighted. After all, she had sung to Finn. She'd picked him. I'd just been there when she'd hatched.

Then she looked at me. She coughed several times. "Papa? Mama?" She said it several times.

Finn's head shot up, and he stared at me. "She's bonded to you, too? It makes sense since you were there when she hatched. You were the first living creature she's seen."

"I'm not sure whether to be flattered or insulted by that remark," I said.

Finn stood carefully, the baby in his arms. "Dragons don't pick anyone. It's not an automatic bonding like it is with some animals. She sensed something special about you, and she knew you'd take care of her."

I felt slightly less offended. "I shouldn't have needed to take care of her if you'd been doing your job."

"Or not hiding a dragon egg in the first place," Zandra muttered.

"I feel terrible that she was alone when she hatched. I protected the box with magic, so nothing could have gotten to her." Finn arched an eyebrow at me. "Well, unless they're Juno and can break my wards with a paw swipe."

"Finn, take this as a sign," Zandra said. "You don't know how to look after a hatchling. What if the next mistake you make kills her?"

"No! I know what I'm doing. I've been reading up on how to become the perfect parent." He wrapped his wings protectively around the dragon. A few seconds later, they started to smoke, so he flapped his wings to prevent any fire. "I'll figure things out. She's safe with me. She wouldn't have sung to me if she didn't think I could look after her."

"You may be able to care for her whilst she's small but how will you keep a hulking great dragon in your bachelor pad?" I asked.

"Um... I was working on a plan. I thought I had more time." Finn's enraptured gaze remained on the hatchling as he cooed and kissed her.

I sidled past him and hopped onto Zandra's shoulder. "He's in dragon thrall. There's nothing we can do to change his mind about letting her go."

"A visit from the dragon's actual parents will do that." Zandra shook her head. "This is a problem I'm not sure how to solve."

"Our list of challenges keeps growing. Binky just handed me interesting information on another murder suspect," I said.

"Who?"

"Someone we already had our eyes on. It's time to interrogate Augustus Dray."

"What about Percival? We know he argued with Hortense not long before she died."

I sighed. "So many suspects, so little time."

"Add in a dragon hatchling, and we won't be chilling with our feet up anytime soon."

Chapter 12

Volunteering viper

We spent an hour with Finn, making a fireproof pen in Vorana's backyard for the baby. When the hatchling was secured and fast asleep, and Sage put on guard duty outside, we had to go our separate ways for work. But during our first break, we went suspect hunting. There may be a baby dragon to take care of, but there was still a killer on the loose, and we sought a suspect to grill.

I sat on Zandra's shoulder as she drove along the main street, looking for signs of Percival and his camera. It wasn't the safest position, but it gave me an excellent vantage point.

"It is curious why he's still here," Zandra said. "Dawn could have a point. He needs to stay around to cover his tracks and make sure no one is looking at him for the crime."

"Or he's still working. He could have another job," I said.

"What's worth filming in Crimson Cove?"

I inspected the tidy storefronts. "It's a pleasant enough town. I've always considered it up and coming. But so long as he doesn't catch accidental footage of baby dragons, that's all I care about."

"Don't care too much. We're not keeping her." Zandra's tone left no room for negotiation.

"I know! I want to make sure she's happy, though."

"We have to act fast with this dragon issue. Rumors spread quickly, and if anyone learns Vorana's got a baby dragon in her backyard, we'll be in trouble. And when the dragons arrive and claim what's theirs, there'll be nothing we can do to stop them. Not even you."

I inspected a paw. "I wouldn't say that."

"Yeah? You're a dragon slayer, now?"

"When needs must. But I prefer to negotiate rather than slay them. Although I fear Finn isn't above fighting a dragon. He didn't want to leave the hatchling this morning."

"And he only did because I pushed him on what he'd tell Cythera about missing work. It's not like he can ask for parental leave to take care of his newborn." Zandra slowed the van, and we studied a guy with a sturdy pot belly. It wasn't Percival.

I leaned against her head. "We'll watch over Finn and make sure he does nothing too foolish."

We stopped outside Sorcha's café and went in to grab food. The place was bustling with regulars, and the delectable scent of frying sausage drifted in the air. Zandra chatted with Sorcha while I inspected the menu. It was full of delicious meaty goodness. Just what a growing cat needed.

"Stop drooling. I know where Percival is." Zandra headed to the door, carrying a brown paper bag.

I followed her, and we climbed into the van. "Sorcha's gossip grapevine is working again?"

"Like a charm. Percival is at the beach!"

We drove the short distance to the pebbled beach, and Zandra parked.

"I recognize that van," she said. "I parked next to it at the sanctuary. It belongs to Percival."

We climbed out and headed to the boardwalk. Percival stood with his camera on his shoulder as he took panoramic shots of the beach, the waves hissing gently along the stones, leaving behind a bubbly foam.

"Greetings!" I called out. "It's Percival, isn't it?"

He turned, the camera still on his shoulder. "Sure. Can I help you with something?"

Zandra made the introductions. "We're working with Angel Force, looking into what happened to Hortense at the animal sanctuary. You were there filming, weren't you?"

Percival lowered the camera and set it down. "I was. Mystical Morsels sent here me to film the reopening of the bakery, do interviews, crowd shots, that sort of thing. They said they're supporting the sanctuary, so wanted additional footage."

"Now that's over, you're still here?" I asked.

"I work freelance, so I take whatever jobs I can. I got offered a commission to get footage of pretty areas. You know, the typical bland piece that makes people want to move to your town and push up the prices."

"That doesn't sound appealing to the locals who live here," I said.

He shrugged. "I go where the work is. I don't question the buyer's ethics. Now, I need to get on."

"Just a few more questions," I said. "How well did you know Hortense?"

"I didn't. I barely spoke to the woman."

"But she spoke to you a few times?"

Percival shook his head. "If she did, I don't remember. I speak to a lot of people at things like this. Everyone's got questions about the equipment or if they can be interviewed. It gets boring, but I'm used to it."

"You didn't argue with Hortense?" Zandra asked.

"Why would I argue with a stranger?" He picked up his camera and turned his back to us.

"Hortense didn't hassle you because you tried to get her on film?" I remained on Zandra's shoulder as she walked around and stood in front of Percival, blocking his view.

He sighed. "Maybe she did. Some people are weird about being on camera. Maybe she thought she wasn't photogenic. It's not a unique issue. When people don't want to be filmed, I don't film them. End of story."

"It wasn't just that, was it?" I asked. "Hortense had an issue with you. She damaged some of your equipment."

Percival tensed then turned as someone called his name. A guy in his early twenties, wearing skinny jeans and a T-shirt with a lanyard around his neck hurried over.

"I brought your coffee," he said.

"What took you so long?" Percival snatched a mug from his hand. "And where's the edited footage from earlier today? You were supposed to have checked it an hour ago."

"I was working on it when you sent me to get coffee."

Percival waved the mug in the air. "Now, I have my coffee, so what are you waiting for? Get on with your job."

The guy backed away then turned and hurried off.

Percival shook his head. "That's the third assistant we've had in four months. I don't see him lasting, either. You need nerves of steel for this job. Max's nerves are made of unset jelly."

"Filming pretty settings requires nerves of steel?" I asked. "It's not as if you're recording in a war zone."

Percival scowled at me. "You need focus and skill to get expert footage. Get it wrong, and you've wasted a whole day and have to start again. That's not cheap. It's also dull to keep filming the same thing."

"Getting back to your fight with Hortense," Zandra said, "why did you conceal your problem with her?"

"I didn't! I don't have to like everyone I meet. All I wanted to do was get decent shots, but she kept interfering, telling me where I couldn't film. She acted as if she owned the town." He took a sip of his coffee and spat it out. "Max! Get back here. I ordered a flat white with one sugar. What's this?"

Max hopped out of the van and ran over. "Sorry! It's what I asked for."

Percival dropped the coffee onto the stones, and it splashed on Max's trainers. "Get me another one. Do I need to write the order down this time or can you remember? Flat white. One sugar. Repeat it back to me."

"Sorry, sorry. Of course not. I got it. Flat white with one sugar. I'll go back into town now." Max turned and ran off.

"Littering is an offense," I said. "Pick up that coffee mug."

Percival scowled as he grabbed the mug. "It's biodegradable."

"You still haven't answered the question," Zandra said.

I twitched my whiskers and fixed Percival with a steely glare. "Anyone would think you're deflecting."

Percival smirked. "I'm used to pushy people in my line of work. I'm often around celebrities and influential types. Most of them are the same. They have giant egos that need to be handled in a particular way. Weirdly, Hortense was like that. When I questioned her about her entitled behavior, she got uppity. So, I ignored her. No point negotiating with irrelevant types."

"Is that when she damaged your equipment?" I asked.

He drew in a sharp breath. "How do you know about that?"

"Is it?"

Percival shrugged. "She grabbed some recording kit and threw it on the ground. This stuff costs a fortune. I'd have sued her if I hadn't been able to repair it. She messed with my livelihood. Fortunately, I carry spare parts, so I could fix the damaged bit."

"That must have made you angry," Zandra said. "Angry enough to have confronted Hortense when no one else was around?"

"I see where you're going with this, but you can get that idea out of your heads. I didn't like the woman, but I didn't stab her with a hayfork. I was working."

"Were you with anyone at the time Hortense was discovered?" I asked.

"Sure was. You see that sweet little presenter over there?" He pointed to a woman with short blonde hair, who stood looking out at the waves. "She's new to the team. We were running through some recording tech stuff together. I won't bore you with the details because it'll be over your heads. Cheri's always finding reasons to spend time with me, if you know what I mean. She can't get enough of me."

"I can see why," I said.

Percival hefted the camera back onto his shoulder. "I need to get to work. Where's that idiot with my coffee?"

I looked at Zandra, and she shook her head. We were done with this guy. But while we were here, it made sense to check his alibi, so while Percival strode off to get more footage, we walked over to Cheri.

She turned as she heard us approaching. Her gaze went to me, and her eyes widened. "Oh! You're lovely. Are you one of those rare Manx cats?"

"Greetings! No, I'm not a Manx, but I'm a rare, extremely magical, powerful familiar who's bonded to the most wonderful witch you'll ever have the pleasure of meeting. I'm Juno and this is Zandra," I said. "We work with Angel Force."

Cheri briefly nodded a greeting at Zandra, but her brilliant blue eyes were focused on me. "Are you sure? I was reading an article about that rare breed of cat. There are only one hundred and fifty left in the wild, and you look just like the one in the photograph. Although, the pictures I saw showed the cats as much fluffier."

"I'm going through a shedding phase. We're here to ask you—"

Cheri clapped her hands together. "I have a brilliant idea. Let me interview you! And we could do a DNA test and see if your ancestry reveals a genetic link to the Manx."

"Why would you want to interview Juno and test her DNA?" Zandra asked.

"Haven't you seen the program, 'DNA Delights and Frights'? It's all the rage in the magical community. People are unearthing connections to famous witches, dark magic-using warlocks, and all sorts of fascinating genetic discoveries that turn families on their heads."

"That sounds like it would cause drama," I said.

"Exactly! People love to watch reality drama. It makes them feel better about their own tangled lives."

"We don't watch much TV," Zandra said. "We're more into movies."

Cheri waved her hands around. "Please say you'll take a slot on the show. People would love to listen to your story. I expect it's fascinating. And even if it isn't, we can make up a few things for creative expression. I could make you a star."

"I'm famous enough," I said. "And my lack of tail is new. I wasn't born this way, so I'm certain I'm not one of your rare fluffy cats."

"Oh, that's disappointing. How about you?" She looked at Zandra. "What family secrets could I extract from your DNA?"

"Count me out. I know enough about my messy family's history and don't want to know any more. But we have some questions for you."

"We freelance with Angel Force," I said. "We were just talking to your charming camera operator, Percival."

"What's he been up to now?" She wrinkled her nose and kicked a small piece of seaweed.

"Are you two close?"

"I stay as far away from Percival as I can. He has... a reputation."

"For being a massive jerk?" Zandra asked.

Cheri lifted her head and grinned. "You're an excellent judge of character. The guy's a nightmare. We only keep him around because he's good with a camera. Actually, he's great. He has this knack with angles that make anybody look good. If he didn't have that talent, he'd have been put on the 'do not hire' list a long time ago."

"You're not in a relationship with him?" I asked.

Surprised laughter shot out of Cheri's mouth. "Hardly! I can barely be in the same room with the guy for more than two minutes before I want to smack him. Did he tell you we're dating?"

"He mentioned you had an interest in him."

"That moron. I'm happily married." She flashed her ring finger. "Even if I wasn't, I'd never go after Percival."

"He said you were together the evening Hortense Scornbloom's body was discovered," Zandra said. "Can you remember that?"

Cheri's forehead furrowed. "No, that's not true. Max, can I borrow you for a minute?"

A harassed-looking Max was returning with more coffee. "Sure. What is it? I got you another caramel syrup latte with extra foam."

"Thanks, hon. The evening that woman was found dead in the barn at the animal sanctuary, we were looking over the filming schedule, weren't we?"

Max nodded. "Yeah. You wanted changes because you weren't sure the weather would be good. We both heard the scream and went to look."

"Was Percival with us?"

Max grimaced. "He'd wandered off to take crowd footage. I hadn't seen him for a while."

"That's what I thought. No, he definitely wasn't with us when Hortense was discovered. Why do you want to know?" Cheri asked.

"We're putting together everyone's movements for that evening," I said. "We want to make sure nothing's been missed."

"There's a story behind that innocent remark." Cheri clasped her takeout mug. "May I interview you about Hortense? I can sell the piece to the local news. An insider scoop from Angel Force would be worth something. But we need to do it now before Hortense's murder becomes old news."

"No interviews at this time," Zandra said. "Not while the investigation is ongoing."

"You two are full of disappointments. No interview for the DNA show, no interview about the murder. There must be something juicy I can get out of you."

"We're dull," I said. "We're your average witch and her boring familiar."

Zandra side-eyed me and winked. "We couldn't be any duller. Every day is the same old, same old. Nothing exciting ever happens in Crimson Cove. Not to us, anyway."

"Oh, well, no harm in asking." Cheri turned to Max. "Has Percival found that piece of camera equipment yet?"

"No. He made me turn the van inside out looking for it. He must have left it somewhere when we were in town."

"He'd better find it. He borrowed it from our kit, and I'll take the money to replace it out of his pay if it doesn't show up soon." She looked back at us and smiled. "Is there anything else?"

"No. Thanks for your time," I said. We walked up the beach and back to the van.

"What do you think of the less than pleasant Percival?" Zandra fished her keys from her pocket.

"There's more to him than meets the eye," I said. "He lied about his alibi, and he tried to hide his argument with Hortense."

"And that she damaged his equipment," Zandra said. "I wonder if the missing bit of kit has something to do with her, too."

"I suspect Percival thought the same thing. He could have confronted her in the barn, and things got rough."

"The guy has a temper," Zandra said.

"And he has no manners. He seems the entitled one from the way he bossed around Max and made out every woman on the planet adored him."

Zandra leaned against the van and looked back at the beach. "Have we found our new prime suspect?"

"Perhaps. But how do we prove it was him?"

Chapter 13

Tasty clue

After an afternoon spent at animal control, we needed something delicious to eat before heading to Angel Force and updating Finn and Cythera on our new prime suspect.

We waited five minutes before being served at Gingerbread Bakery. Word must have gotten out that Tia had reopened, and everyone was dropping by to sample the goods and congratulate her on her stunning new bakery.

We reached the front of the queue, and she grinned at us. "What'll it be?"

I had my booping snooter pressed against the glass, so I didn't miss any goodies. "We'll take a dozen pink frosted fancies, six iced cherry tarts, and a dozen—"

"We'll have two of whatever you think we'd like," Zandra said. "Well, whatever Finn and I will like, unless you've started making salmon-flavored cake for a certain fussy feline familiar."

"It's still not a fan favorite." Tia smiled at me. "Sorry, Juno. No salmon."

"It's an underserved market. You'd make a fortune if you made the first sweet salmon cake. It could be like a mousse, but with sweet sponge layers." I licked my lips so I wouldn't drool on the clean floor.

Tia poked out her tongue. "I'll consider it, but no promises."

"Sweet is good. But we need to keep the angels happy," I said. "If we show up with nothing to eat, Cythera will be grumpy."

"Fine. A box of regular glazed donuts. Let's not go overboard, or Cythera will get suspicious of us," Zandra said.

"You're working with them on the murder?" Tia placed the donuts in a takeout box and added two dark chocolate and cherry brownies.

"We need to ensure they didn't go down any wrong alleys in this investigation," I said. "Especially since they've been looking at you and Binky."

Tia shook her head. "I thought I was in trouble. Cythera wouldn't let up with the questioning. When she found out I'd argued with Hortense, it got worse."

"What did you fight about?" Zandra asked.

"This place. Hortense wanted to buy the building and the land!"

"She had dreams of running a bakery?" I asked.

"No! She wanted to open an exotic pet store. I told her she'd never get a license. Pet stores aren't popular. Too many of them are run by shady people who want to turn a profit rather than ensure the animals' welfare, but she wouldn't listen. She said there was a niche market for certain species."

"She got super mean." Binky's head appeared from under the counter. "I had to show her my teeth before she left."

"Where would Hortense have gotten the money to buy this place?" I asked.

"I didn't quiz her about it because it made no difference to me," Tia said. "I'll never give up the bakery. I love living here and running my business. Hortense said everyone had their price, and she'd find mine. She even offered to set me up in a new bakery. Apparently, she had contacts and could have gotten me a manager's job in a franchise. I wasn't interested. I've got bigger plans."

"I've heard you're considering expanding if things go well," I said.

"It's early days, but I think I've got it right with Gingerbread. It's cozy and welcoming, and everyone loves the food. Even Hortense admitted I made the most amazing scones she'd ever tasted. Although giving her a free scone didn't improve her mood."

"Even though Hortense was mean enough for us to want to hurt her, we were together when she was attacked," Binky said. "I walked to the sanctuary with Tia and then had a sniff around, but she was in my sights the whole time. Besides, if Tia ever feels the urge to kill, I'll do it for her so she won't need to get her hands dirty. She'll always be innocent."

"Don't say that! Especially not in front of Angel Force. We've only just convinced Cythera we weren't involved." Tia glanced at me and Zandra.

"I trust both of you," I said, "and we're not Angel Force. We're pursuers of justice only in our spare time. The rest of the time, justice must take care of itself."

"Can you think of any reason why someone wanted Hortense dead?" Zandra asked. "Was she going after any other businesses, trying to get the owners to sell their properties, too?"

"Not that I know of. Hortense didn't say she had any other places she was interested in, but it's possible. She saw this as an ideal opportunity. She came in when the place was still being renovated and said I could stop, and she'd finish the rest. Make it her own."

"It's another motive," I said. "Hortense could have been hassling other businesses. There are powerful magic users around here, and she could have picked on the wrong person."

"So why not zap her in the butt with a spell rather than run her through with a hayfork?" Zandra said.

Tia leaned across the counter. "From the rumors I've been hearing, that's not what killed Hortense. Do you know about the pasty shoved down her throat?"

I nodded. "The angels think her killer put it there after she was stabbed. She must have been on the ground, bleeding out, when they did it."

Tia shuddered, her expression shifting to worried. "That's gruesome. You don't think they were trying to frame me, do you? I've just started stocking pasties as part of my sponsorship deal with Mystical Morsels. Maybe the killer saw me fighting with Hortense and thought I'd be an easy target to frame."

"If anyone tries to frame you, I'll batter them with my murder mittens." Binky growled.

Tia leaned down and kissed Binky's head. "Such a sweetie. I'd do the same for you."

"It's something we can ask the suspects," I said.

"Other people would have overheard our argument. We raised our voices," Tia said. "Hortense's killer could have used that to their advantage to distract attention from them."

"We'll get to the bottom of this." Zandra paid for the food. "I'll keep the angels off your back, too. We've received new information about a suspect that should lead to an arrest soon."

Tia's eyes widened. "Who is it? Can you tell me?"

"We shouldn't say," I said, "but if it was him, then he deserves everything that's coming his way."

Tia raised her eyebrows then nodded. "Say no more. I'll be glad when this is over. Having just reopened, I don't want a murder associated with my bakery."

"I'll bite anyone who lies about you being a killer," Binky said.

"Binky, we've talked about this. No biting unless it's an emergency."

"I'd consider saving Gingerbread Bakery an emergency," I said. "Bite away, Binky."

"Please, don't encourage her," Tia muttered.

We said goodbye and headed out of the bakery toward the pizza parlor, where we grabbed two large triple cheese and pepperoni pizzas then walked to Angel Force.

The office was subdued, with only a few angels around. Even Cythera's office was empty, which was unusual. She often worked late into the evening.

Finn stepped out of the kitchen, a mug in his hand. "Hey, glad you're both here. And you brought food! Even better. Is that pepperoni I smell?"

"With triple cheese. We thought we'd bring dinner." Zandra set down the pizza boxes.

"I'm starved. I've barely had time to eat today." He flipped open the lid of the pizza box and snagged the largest slice.

"How's your new scaled arrival settling into her home?" I glanced around, but no one was paying us attention.

Finn grinned, flushed with the joy of being a new father. "Sage is checking in every hour. My baby is settling well. She's happy, and Vorana is feeding her. I've been by twice, and she's looking good."

"Have you decided what to do with her?"

Finn lowered his pizza slice. "Still thinking about it."

"Don't think for too long, or the dragons won't give you a choice," I whispered.

He grimaced. "I know! I'm on it."

"Where's Cythera?" I asked.

"Maverick showed up half an hour ago and insisted they go out for the evening," Finn said. "She wasn't happy, but he can be persuasive and isn't put off by her grumpiness. He's taking her to dinner so they can discuss their honeymoon."

"Maverick's a good influence on her," I said. "The relationship gives Cythera something to focus on other than work and her intense dislike of me."

Finn chuckled as he took more pizza. "She is envious of your amazing detection skills."

"Did she tell you that?" I ate a piece of pepperoni from Zandra's slice.

"Not in those exact words, but that's the reason she gives you such a hard time." He took another bite of his pizza, a smile on his face. Food always made Finn happy.

"We've been digging," Zandra said. "And we've found a few things that could be of interest."

"The investigation is on the whiteboard. You can fill in the blanks if you like." Finn dropped into a chair and lifted his feet onto the desk.

"Cythera won't mind us defacing her precious whiteboard?" I walked to the board and looked up at it. All the suspects' names were listed there.

"I'll tell her it was me. Just make sure your handwriting is messy."

"No problems there." Zandra took the cap off a black pen.

"I'm glad to see you have Tia and Binky listed as innocent," I said.

"That took persuading on my part," Finn said. "Cythera is suspicious of both of them. She knows Tia argued with Hortense."

"We stopped by the bakery on our way here." I walked over and rested a paw on the donut box. "Tia said Hortense wouldn't give up her interest in buying the business. She wanted to open an exotic pet store."

Finn nodded. "Exotic pets for sale around here would raise hackles."

"Where would you even get the animals from?" Zandra asked. "Import them from other countries?"

"It would never have happened," Finn said. "We have too much respect for familiars to see wild animals stuck in cages to be poked at by curious visitors. We don't even have a zoo. We like our critters wild and free."

"I don't like to raise this point, but if I didn't know Tia and Binky so well, I'd say they had a solid motive for murder. Let's deflect Cythera away from Tia and Binky if she returns to them as suspects," I said.

"Already working on it. And you see, I'm up there, too. Thankfully, also listed as innocent, even though I wasn't Hortense's biggest fan," Finn said. "Cythera can be stubborn at times, but she knows what she's doing. What's the new information you've got?"

"It's about Percival Thornfield," Zandra said. "We talked to him. To begin with, he lied about arguing with Hortense, but then he revealed all. He's not a nice guy."

"Percival is vile," I said. "He was rude to his assistant and lied about the presenter, Cheri, being attracted to him."

"But most importantly, he faked an alibi," Zandra said. "He claimed he was with Cheri the evening Hortense was killed. She says otherwise. Cheri was with Max, the crew's assistant, and Percival was nowhere to be seen."

Finn set down his pizza crust and licked his fingers. "Interesting. Percival told me the same thing. Cheri wasn't around at the time, so I couldn't check on his alibi. They really weren't together?"

"They weren't. And some of his equipment has gone missing," I said. "We think Hortense stole it to punish him."

"And Percival confronted her and demanded its return?" Finn sat forward in his seat.

"Since the guy has a temper and Hortense caused him trouble, it may have pushed him over the edge. They argued, and he grabbed the hayfork and attacked her," Zandra said.

"It's looking more likely Percival did it," I said. "We just need his confession."

"Evidence and an eye witness would also be helpful." Finn sighed. "And given what you told me about Dawn and her hidden stash of cash, she's not in the clear."

"On your amazing magical whiteboard, it shows Augustus is Dawn's alibi," I said. "Although we've been hearing less than sweet things about him."

"Like what?"

"He's a gossip."

"Oh! Yeah, don't share secrets with Augustus." Finn shook his head. "He's volunteering tomorrow, so I'll speak to him. And he's had run-ins with Hortense, too, so I haven't discounted him from this investigation."

"Everyone has had a run-in with Hortense," I said. "They can't all be murder suspects!"

"Some people bring out the worst in others," Finn said.

"What'll you do about the money Dawn was hiding?" I asked.

"That's tricky. If her alibi checks out, then the money isn't connected to what happened to Hortense, so it's not relevant."

"Where did she get it from?" Zandra asked. "You don't pay your volunteers, do you?"

"They get an allowance for training and their travel expenses paid if they need it. They also get fed while working, but that's it," Finn said. "I couldn't afford to run the place if I had to pay staff."

"You'll be able to now you have your new pasty patron from Mystical Morsels," I said.

He smiled and nodded. "I must get onto that. I haven't had a moment to myself with the murder and becoming a father. I don't want Celeste to think I'm not interested."

"Parenthood is never easy," I said. "But if you don't act quickly with that young dragon, you may not get a chance to experience fatherhood for real."

He shuffled around in his seat. "Yeah, yeah. There's no need to keep nagging."

"There's every need," Zandra said. "If you start a war with the dragons, we won't stand by your side and defend you."

He pouted. "You'd abandon me because I made a dubious life choice?"

"Probably not," I said. "Zandra went through a phase of wearing a baseball cap around the wrong way, and I'm still with her. But you must act swiftly with that hatchling. Sage is furious the baby is staying in Vorana's backyard, and I'm taking the brunt of her displeasure."

"I didn't mean to get anyone else messed up in this. I will fix things, I promise."

My gaze ran over the suspect list. "The sooner we get this murder cleared up, the better. Then you can focus on fatherhood and dragons."

Finn pinched his chin between his thumb and finger. "I'll speak to Dawn tomorrow and see if I can get any information about that money."

"It should be simple to get the information out of her," I said. "She's sweet on you."

He chuckled. "Good one, Juno."

"I'm not joking."

Finn's eyes grew wide. "What makes you say that?"

"She told us it's the reason Hortense didn't like her. Dawn kept flirting with you, and Hortense got jealous," Zandra said.

"Dawn never flirted with me! I'm much older than her. And as for Hortense..."

"She's too old for you?" I smirked.

He blushed. "Yeah. And pricklier than an angry porcupine. Dawn's just a kid. I see her as a sister, so I'd never go there. And Hortense, no way. I always got a headache when I spent too much time with her." Finn rose from his seat and paced the office. "There was no flirting. Dawn never flirted with anyone. Her default mode is anger and suspicion."

"Why would she tell us that?" Zandra asked.

"Maybe it was a cover?" I said. "Dawn wanted to distract us from the real reason Hortense disliked her."

"That reason being related to the money you found?"

There was a ping from Finn's computer. "The background check on Hortense is back. It's taken a while to come through."

We gathered around the computer as he opened the document and read through the information.

"She's got no criminal history," he said after a couple of minutes. "No alerts against her name or any weird search histories that should have us worried."

"Scroll up," I said. "Look! Hortense worked at Mystical Morsels."

"She never mentioned working there in her volunteering application," Finn said. "I'd have remembered."

"Why hide that?" Zandra asked.

"Something bad must've happened," I said. "Maybe Hortense was fired. She has no new employer listed since she left the job at Mystical Morsels six months ago."

Finn scanned the information. "I could get in touch with Celeste. She was helpful at the opening event, so she may know Hortense."

"Celeste said she didn't know her," I said.

"She probably doesn't. It's a massive company. But she could put me in touch with the right person to interview." Finn pulled up Celeste's contact information. "Do you want in if I can get someone to speak to about Hortense?"

I nodded. "So long as they bring free pasties, we're in."

Chapter 14

Dating difficulties

"That's the final report filed." Zandra pushed away from the desk she'd been sitting at for an hour. "You ready to grab lunch, and then we'll go to the interview at Angel Force?"

"I never say no to an early lunch. But give me five minutes. Sammy only had a half-day in rehab, and I want to see how he got on." I unfolded from the pile of paperwork I'd been keeping warm and hopped onto the floor.

"Do you think he's making progress?"

"He's more stable but has work to do before he trusts his magic. He's quiet, though. And he keeps apologizing to me."

"Sammy has a lot to apologize for."

"None of what happened was his fault."

Zandra tilted her head from side to side. "I like Sammy. You two were sweet together, but he underestimates himself. That cat has power, but he's too scared to use it."

I didn't like arguing with my witch, but I needed to defend Sammy. "I know how that feels. You want to do your best, but you don't want to risk harming anyone."

"Your magic isn't unstable. It's unique. And it's always changing. No wonder you worry about firing up the wrong spell in case you blow someone up. I don't know how you keep a handle on it. It must be like waking up as a new person every week strapped into a rollercoaster you're not sure you want to ride."

"But ride it I do." I lifted my chin. "I'm not that bad. And what's wrong with having a unique familiar?"

"I didn't say there was anything wrong with it. It just makes life trickier. And you know me, I'm all for the easy life."

"The safe life," I muttered.

"What was that?"

"Have you given any more thought to dating Randal again?"

Zandra smirked at me. "You can change the subject all you like, but you know I'm right."

"I'm going to the animal pens." I stalked away. Zandra made a valid point about my magic, just as she did with Sammy. I'd seen glimpses of his true power, but his fear held him back, just as it did me. There must be a compromise in this situation. A way everyone could be happy.

I entered the room at the back of the building where the animal pens were kept. Sammy sat in his usual pen, his paws tucked neatly underneath him, and his eyes almost closed. He opened them and blinked at me.

"How did your session go?" I walked over to him.

"Good, I think. I need to rest. It was intense. My tail is still twitching."

"You smell better."

"Less toxic?"

"It's an improvement. I'm glad you're healing."

"I'm feeling more myself. I just need to get rid of all this guilt. It's churning in my gut like a rotten rodent."

I sniffed the treats left inside his cage. "Guilt is a selfish emotion. If you feel guilty, you're thinking only of how you're feeling and not the other people involved."

His eyes widened. "I've never thought about it that way."

I sighed. "Feel guilty if you like, but think about what good it does you. Does feeling guilty make you productive and try hard? If it does, then feel as guilt-ridden as you like. Roll around in that gray gooey guilt bubble. But if feeling guilty makes you defeated as you drag around a sense of hopelessness you'll never shed, lose the guilt. Focus on what you can do right now. That's the important thing."

Sammy was quiet for a moment.

I continued, "I know what happened to you wasn't your fault."

"I held back. It doesn't help that I have no bond, so my magic is always looking for someone to latch onto. It latched onto the wrong people."

"I should have realized something was wrong with you."

"Now who's feeling guilty?"

We touched noses through the bars, and I inhaled his slightly less sour aroma.

"No one is perfect," I said.

"You come close."

"Sometimes. But there are things I need to work on. We always need to work on improving ourselves."

Sammy glanced over my shoulder. "Like your tail? You never told me what happened to it."

I stiffened. "I'm going through some changes."

"It must be the stress. Your fur is falling out, too."

I was only too aware I was shedding, and I was glad Tinkerbell wasn't here to mock me in her usual charmless way.

"You ready?" Zandra poked her head around the door. "If we're late for the interview, Cythera won't be pleased. She'll be like an officious usher at the theater and not let us in once the door is closed."

"You're still working on solving the murder?" Sammy asked. "I've been hearing about it from Barney."

"We think we've got our man, but we're following up on some new information. It won't be long now until the case is solved, then you'll have my complete attention."

"Let's hustle," Zandra said.

"Got to go." I hurried out of the room and along the corridor with Zandra. The main door opened in front of us, and Randal walked in. His gaze locked with Zandra's, and he blushed.

"Oh! Hey, it's good to see you. I've been meaning to catch up since our... date."

Zandra turned beetroot red. "Oh, that. It wasn't a date. I mean, was it? You got me coffee and then we mucked out barns."

Randal glanced down at me. "No! Of course, I didn't ask you to go with me when the bakery opened. But it was good to hang out. Perhaps we could do it again?"

"Um... We could. Work's busy, though, and—"

"Zandra would love to accompany you on a proper date. We'll leave you to make the arrangements, Randal. Don't we have murder suspects to interview?" I asked Zandra.

"Sure! See you around." She hurried past Randal and out the door.

I nodded at him. "Don't worry. We'll make this happen." I dashed after Zandra.

She looked down at me as we hurried toward Angel Force. "Not a word."

"I was going to say how well Randal looked."

"Sure, you were. And I'm going to say dating is hard."

I considered my complicated situation with Sammy and had to agree.

We arrived at Angel Force with seconds to spare. I was surprised to see Celeste being shown into the interview room by Finn. They seemed friendly as she chatted and smiled at something Finn said to her. Cythera was saying goodbye to Maverick.

He strode past us, a big smile on his face. "We're spending the evening sampling wedding cake. What a treat. I intend to have a big slice of everything."

"Have fun," I said.

"When I'm with my dear Cythera, that's all I have." He nodded at both of us then left the office.

"Hey, you two. We're about to get started," Finn said from the interview room door. "You know the drill." He pointed at the room next door with the large one-way mirror and speakers that allowed us to see and hear everything.

We dashed in and got settled in a seat while Cythera ran through the formal interview opening, getting Celeste's details.

"We appreciate you taking the time out of your busy day," Finn said.

"It was my pleasure. I've been meaning to visit again to talk about what we can offer your sanctuary. And I wanted to see Tia and ensure she was happy with how things are going. I may be the boss, but I like to show I'm a person, too."

"Cythera should follow that philosophy," I murmured.

Zandra settled me onto her lap and stroked my fur.

"You're the CEO of Mystical Morsels, is that correct?" Cythera asked.

Celeste had a hand resting on her mobile snow globe. "That's right. I've been there for eighteen months."

"Do you enjoy your work?"

"Very much. In that time, I've established lucrative partnerships, including the one in Crimson Cove. I'm delighted we can be a part of your community."

"Am I right in thinking Hortense Scornbloom worked at your company?"

Celeste's eyes widened a fraction. "It's a big place, and we have dozens of offices. I'd have to check the records." Her mobile globe had been buzzing almost non-stop since she'd settled into her seat.

Cythera glared at the buzzing equipment. "Can you put that on silent while we talk?"

"Sorry, as I explained to Finn, I'm waiting for a call from an international client. If I miss it, it could jeopardize a deal I've been working on for almost six months."

"I said it was okay," Finn said. "Celeste was happy to stop by and answer our questions, so I didn't see the harm in making a compromise. We don't want Mystical Morsels missing out on something big."

"Then we'll make this quick," Cythera said. "We contacted your Human Resources team and learned Hortense worked directly for you, providing administrative support."

"They did know each other?" I leaned closer to the glass.

Celeste opened her mouth, but nothing came out for several seconds. "I have a number of people who do that."

"You must know them all," Finn said. "I expect they're in and out of your office several times a day."

"Some of them are." Celeste's globe buzzed again, and she checked it briefly. "This is embarrassing to admit because I insist on the highest professional standards in the company. I... I shouldn't have concealed this from you."

"Go on," Cythera said.

Celeste released her grip on her mobile snow globe and adjusted the cuffs of her tidy white blouse. "I briefly dated Hortense. I've been keeping quiet because it would raise questions about my work ethic. As the head of the company, I have power. If other members of staff learned I dated an administrator, they may think I manipulated her into doing so. Which I didn't."

"Whoa! I didn't see that coming," Zandra said.

I was leaning so close to the glass, my booping snooter almost touched it. "Same here. It makes sense why Celeste would want to keep that juicy secret quiet."

"You lied to us about knowing the victim?" Cythera asked.

"Not for any reason related to what happened to her," Celeste said. "We went on a few dates, but it was never serious. I like a person who speaks their mind, and Hortense was never afraid to do that. She told me a few home truths, and I respected her for it."

"Why didn't the relationship continue?" Finn asked.

"Hortense was too blunt. After a few dates, I realized she had no social filter. She said whatever she wanted to whomever she wanted, and she didn't care about the consequences. There was an embarrassing incident in a restaurant that made me cool things off."

Finn made a few notes on the pad in front of him. "How did Hortense react?"

"In her usual way. She said she wasn't interested in me anyway and was curious to see what kind of person I was outside of the office. She told me she'd been underwhelmed by our dates."

"That must have stung," I murmured.

"Was that why you fired her?" Cythera asked.

"No! Hortense leaving the company had nothing to do with our relationship. She was good at what she did but hugely unpopular. She kept crossing the line with rude comments. Our Human Resources team received numerous complaints about her, and they got so bad that I had no choice but to let her go."

"It must have been a relief when Hortense was out of the picture, so you didn't have to deal with the issue of your failed relationship," Finn said.

"It wasn't a big deal. And I wouldn't even call it a relationship. We had a few dates, things didn't work out, and we moved on. If it had gotten awkward between us, there are plenty of departments I could have relocated her to. Hortense didn't lose her job because we dated. It even ended civilly if you remove her rudeness. But that was just Hortense." A message came in on Celeste's mobile snow globe, which she checked but ignored. "If we're done, I need to get back to work."

"One more thing. Your alibi for the night of Hortense's murder," Finn said.

"I dated the woman! I didn't want her dead."

"I'm sorry to ask, but you were at the animal sanctuary," Finn said. "Could you tell us your movements while you were there?"

Celeste shifted in her seat and frowned. "This is the first time I've ever been accused of killing someone."

"No accusations are being made, but we need to check where everyone was that evening so we can discount them. I'm sure you understand."

"Very well. I was mingling. I spent time with the TV presenter, Cheri, going over the interviews she had planned. After that, I talked to your volunteers. There was a young man with a splendid long beard. There was also a nervous young woman with a deep love for animals. They were all she talked about. I believe her name is Dawn. I was chatting with her a couple of minutes before she discovered Hortense. And I talked to you, Finn."

"I remember. And I appreciate your support at the sanctuary."

Celeste's smile was genuine. "It's my pleasure. It's a wonderful place. I was thrilled when I found it. Grassroots causes are the pillars of communities, and they do so much to help people." Her mobile snow globe buzzed again. "This is the call! If we're finished, I must take it."

"We're done. Thank you for your time." Cythera opened the door and showed her out. Celeste was already talking to someone on her globe as she walked away.

Finn came into our room a few seconds later. "Well, what did you think?"

"The dating angle threw us," Zandra said. "No one knew about that, so Celeste could have kept it a secret."

"She must have figured honesty was the best policy," Finn said.

"Or she was worried we'd find out if we dug around. She didn't want Angel Force questioning her employees," I said.

"I'll ask the volunteers and make sure Celeste was with them," Finn said. "But if she was with Dawn just before Hortense was discovered, she can't be involved. I'm heading to the sanctuary after work. Augustus will be there, so I'll talk to him, too."

I nodded. "We'll join you. We need to do some fact-checking."

"Finn! With me," Cythera called out as she passed the room, ignoring us.

"Duty calls. See you later." He dashed away.

Zandra stood and settled me on her shoulder. "We didn't get food."

"I know. Your stomach was growling so loudly, I thought Cythera would come in and reprimand you. I'm ready to eat. And while we eat, we'll make a plan to uncover the killer."

Chapter 15

Fiery distraction

Zandra set down the note she'd picked up after we'd come in from an afternoon of work. "Finn's got an emergency at the sanctuary. He needs us there ASAP."

"What kind of emergency?" I asked.

She shrugged. "Maybe Augustus confessed, but he's playing hard to get."

I fired up my magic. "I'll get us there."

Zandra rubbed a hand down her pants. "I'm covered in animal excretion. I think it's from the anal glands of that weird beaver who played hard to get."

"Finn's sanctuary is full of animal goo, so you'll fit right in. There's no time to waste. He needs us." I jumped on her shoulder and cast the translocation spell that took us to the sanctuary. When we got there, there was no sign of Finn, so we headed to his office. He wasn't in there either.

"If you're looking for Finn, he's in the end barn. The one with the damaged roof. He must have something wild with him because he ordered us to stay out." Augustus Dray set down the wheelbarrow he'd been pushing.

"Thanks. It's Augustus, isn't it?" I asked.

He nodded. "Something I can do for you?"

"We'll get back to you soon." I pointed a paw in the direction of the end barn, and Zandra ran over. We discovered the door was locked.

"Finn! We got your message," she said as she knocked on the door. "Is everything okay?"

"You alone?"

"It's Juno and me. Can we come in?"

"Give me a minute. Argh! Can you help?" Finn asked.

"Stay there. I'll let them in."

I was surprised to hear Sage's voice on the other side of the door, and her tone was anything but happy. Something heavy was pushed along the floor. Then a few seconds later, Sage's face appeared in a small gap. "Come in. Be quick!"

"What are you doing?" I hopped off Zandra's shoulder so she could slide through the gap easily and then followed her in.

"I brought Finn's demon child back. She tried to burn off Vorana's eyebrows the last time she fed her," Sage said.

"The baby probably belched," Finn said. "Hatchlings get wind if they gulp their food too quickly."

"Other hatchlings don't belch fire when they get gassy! Vorana could have been killed. I can't allow that dragon beast to stay at her home a second longer." Sage stomped back to Finn.

We hurried over to join them. Finn sat in one corner with the dragon hatchling on his lap. The baby was fast asleep, although she stirred as we got near.

"She's cute," Zandra said. "Does she have a name?"

"The Demon Child," Sage said. "Or Fire Starter?"

Finn rolled his eyes. "I want to name her, but if I get too attached and then have to let her go..." He shook his head. "It's best if I don't."

"It was a risk bringing the baby here," I said to Sage. "Dragons have been poking around. They'll catch her scent."

"Better they catch her scent here than lumber around Vorana's backyard and break things they have no business breaking, my witch included," Sage said. "No more baby dragons, Finn. Got it?"

He nodded. "Sorry I made you worry about Vorana. I never meant to put her at any risk."

Sage swirled magic around her and vanished.

The baby stirred, blinked, and spotted me. She leapt in the air, flapping her wing nubs, and lumbered over before launching herself onto my back and chirping her joy.

I staggered under her weight. "You've grown!"

The baby chirruped happily and huffed hot smoke over me before grabbing an ear and sucking it.

"Aww! She adores you," Zandra said.

I struggled to stay on my feet. "Who wouldn't?"

"I know I can't keep her here, but I don't know what else to do." Finn stood and brushed straw off the back of his pants. "I don't suppose—"

"Our basement apartment is no place for this infant," I said. "And if Sage caught us sneaking her back in, you'll be plucked, and I'll lose what little fur I have left."

He lifted a hand. "Just a thought. I'll keep her here for now. But I'll have to move her soon."

"Zandra, you watch the baby. We have a suspect to speak to," I said.

Zandra took a step back. "She won't be happy with me. What if she cries? If there are dragons around, they'll come for her."

"Don't tell me you're afraid of fighting off a few dragons." Finn grinned at Zandra.

"Maybe I should stay." I glowered at Finn. Joking about my witch fighting dragons was off limits.

Zandra waved me away. "Go! We need to get this investigation sorted. I'll cast a barrier spell over the barn while you're gone. That'll deflect any lurking dragons. Don't hang around, though. I'm not used to infants. They cry when I hold them. And they usually puke."

"She's already done that." Finn pointed to a stain on his pants. "I burped her when Sage brought her in."

With some struggle, I transferred the hatchling to Zandra. "I won't be long. Be good for your Auntie Zandra."

I hurried out of the barn with Finn, and we locked the door. Then I stepped back and waited until Zandra's barrier spell was firmly in place. I tested it several times. It was strong.

Finn looked down at me as we headed to talk to Augustus. "You don't have to say anything. I'm a massive idiot, and I've taken on too much, but I don't want to let that baby go."

"You are an idiot, but you're also under her thrall. And I see the appeal."

"I was thinking I should leave town with her for a while. I could raise her somewhere where no one knows us, just until she's strong enough to defend herself. Then she can have a say in where she lives. If she chooses me, the dragons will have no choice but to agree she can remain with me."

"That won't be a fun existence. Are you prepared to run from the dragons for months? They won't stop pursuing you, not now the baby's been born. You've broken a lot of dragon laws, and they'll expect you to pay. Most likely with your life."

"I can make this right. I just need to figure out how."

I shot him a sympathetic look. "We'll figure it out later. We have suspects to quiz."

Finn fluttered his wings then pulled back his shoulders. "Hey, Augustus. Have you got a few minutes?"

"Always for you. What have you been doing? Rolling around in the hay with some lusty young thing? You have stains all over you." Augustus brushed straw off Finn's shoulder.

"Tussling with a creature who doesn't appreciate this is the best place for it. Same old, same old." Finn shrugged and looked shamefaced at lying.

"What have you got in that barn? My curiosity was piqued when you dashed past with something under your wings. I hope you didn't get bitten. Any injuries you need me to tend to? Remove your shirt so I can take a peek." Augustus grinned and winked at me.

"I'm good. But thanks," Finn said.

"Can't blame a guy for trying. If you don't want me to tend to your wounds, what do you need me for?"

"I've been meaning to talk to you about Hortense."

Augustus's eyes widened. "What can I tell you about that old harpy?"

"You didn't like her?" I asked.

"You're a glorious sight for tired eyes. I saw you the evening Hortense the Horrible was staked."

"Juno helps us out now and again," Finn said.

"Us? Angel Force?"

I nodded. "On the tricky cases."

"Oh! I feel faint." Augustus fanned his face. "You're questioning me in an official capacity?"

"It's nothing formal," Finn said. "But someone murdered Hortense, and we need to find out who."

Augustus arched an eyebrow. "And you're coming to me because I know the juicy gossip?"

"And because you were there that evening," I said. "You could have seen something that helps us solve this case."

Augustus pulled out a red spotted handkerchief and dabbed his brow. "Well, as I expect Finn has told you, I love to poke around in other people's business. Everyone has some dirty little secret to hide."

"Did Hortense have any secrets?"

He ran a hand down his beard and then curled the end around his fingers. "Perhaps. What do you need to know?"

"How well did you know Hortense?" Finn asked.

"She had a viper's tongue and the sting of a scorpion. I'm certain her life's motto was 'misery loves company.' She was always trying to bring people down. If she saw a smile on your face, she set herself the task of ensuring it was gone by the end of the day. I expect she awarded herself some prize if she made enough people miserable. Probably a cactus. I imagine she has a room in her home full of spiky plants."

"Did Hortense ever come after you?" Finn asked.

"She took a few swipes at me, but I didn't rise to her gloomy challenge. I preferred to walk away and show she didn't bother me. That made her angrier, but it gave me satisfaction." Augustus inspected the ends of his beard. "I can't say the same for poor little Dawn, though. She bit every time Hortense pushed her."

I twitched my whiskers. "Did they fight the night Hortense died?"

"No! I taught Dawn well. She'd seen the light and realized that splashing hatred over Hortense made her stronger. Ignoring her worked wonders, though. She hated being ignored."

"Did you see Dawn at the sanctuary that evening?" Finn asked.

"Yes, we were together most of the night. She's an adorable little thing, and I've taken her under my wing. Dawn has a tragic past. She's like an injured bird that keeps trying to fly before her wings are strong enough." Augustus sighed. "She's shared a few snippets from her dark times. So much sadness in such a short life. I'm hoping she's turned a corner.

And Dawn loves it here. The sanctuary is helping her."

"Where were you when Hortense was discovered?" I asked.

"I love a party. Any excuse to mingle and get the latest gossip, and I'm there. As I said, I was with Dawn most of the evening. We indulged in the free food and drink. And I spoke to that posh lady who donated the freebies. I can't remember her name, but she wore a gorgeous dress. Cassandra, was it?"

"Celeste Hearthstone. She's the CEO of Mystical Morsels," Finn said.

"That's the one. And if I had curves like that, I'd have my outfits tailored to perfection too." Augustus tugged the sweater he wore. "Still, I make most things look good. It's the broad shoulders, you see." He winked at me again.

"Have you seen Hortense have a run-in with anyone recently?" Finn asked.

Augustus laughed. "You dear thing. I don't have enough fingers and toes to count out that list. And not meaning to sound scandalous, but you'd be on it. You argued with Hortense less than a week ago."

"Fortunately, I have an impeccable alibi." Finn looked down at me. "Anyone else?"

"Tia and her marvelous familiar, Binky. I was in the bakery when Hortense rowed with her. She wouldn't let go. Hortense kept saying to name her price and money was no object. I could tell Tia was embarrassed. She was busy with customers and kept telling Hortense to come back at a better time, but Hortense ignored her. Things got tense until the wondrous Binky escorted Hortense off the premises."

"We've heard about that fight," I said. "Neither of them are involved."

"I'm happy about that. Tia's food is marvelous. Although I'm not a pasty fan. At least, not the ones she's serving. Maybe I got a bad batch, but the last two pasties have been underwhelming." Augustus poked out his tongue. "You should speak to your new friend at Mystical Morsels, Finn. She might give me a discount on my next order. Or a free box of treats for all of us."

"There's no harm in asking," Finn said. "Anyone else?"

Augustus tapped a finger against his chin. "The odious man who was forever sticking his camera in people's faces and asking questions. I don't know his name, but he was at the sanctuary that evening. I suggested he do a personal piece on me and my colorful nomadic lifestyle, and he sneered in my face. The cheek! He said my story wasn't worth telling and nobody would be interested in a wannabe hippie whose beard had seen better days. I was almost offended. I followed him around for fifteen minutes, giving him pointers on how to take better shots. It was amusing to see him get flustered."

"You mean Percival," Finn said.

"I don't know his name, and I don't care to know his name. I called him Odious Ooze after that. It suited him. But I'll tell you this about him. He was as mean as a rattlesnake and even less pleasant than a trodden-on scorpion. If someone couldn't help him, he dismissed them." Augustus glanced around, seeming disappointed he didn't have a bigger audience. "He was even rude to the pretty lady presenter. I didn't hear what she said to him, but he didn't like it. He insulted her then pretended she'd misheard. He walked off, laughing to himself as if he'd done something clever. Rudeness is stupid and cruel."

"Did you see him speak to Hortense at any point in the evening?" I asked.

"I didn't follow him around all night, honey. I had better things to do. Although, it would have been enjoyable to see Hortense and Odious Ooze squabble. Hortense never backed down. She kept going and going until her enemy lay on the floor in a puddle of exhaustion and misery." Augustus cocked a hip and rested one hand on it. "I'm glad she didn't get her way with the bakery. I heard she wanted to open an animal pelt store. Rugs made from skins or something barbaric like that. Disgusting woman."

"I heard it was a pet store," Finn said.

Augustus raised his hands and looked around the sanctuary. "Who'd want to do such a thing when they're involved in a glorious place like this? Every time I deal with people, it makes me realize why I stick with animals."

"You can't go wrong with spending quality time with fine felines," I said.

"Quite right. At least you're easy to read. We know when you're hungry, cold, or need to empty your bowels. There are few animals in the kingdom as deceitful as people. Those that are, are most closely related to us. And that's no good thing. We can be sly and sneaky."

"Thanks, Augustus. I appreciate your time," Finn said.

He held out his hands. "No handcuffs? I'd enjoy being restrained and frisked by you. What if I tell you I've been a bad boy?"

Finn shook his head. "Go on, now. Doesn't that wheelbarrow full of food need to be somewhere?"

Augustus laughed as he strode away.

Finn smiled. "I should have warned you about Augustus's flirty side."

"No warning needed. He was fun. And it means Dawn has an alibi."

"And so do Augustus and Celeste," Finn said.

"So, we focus on Percival. Everyone we've talked to had nothing good to say about him. And he's proven himself a liar."

"It looks like we have our guy. But we need to gather enough evidence to arrest him," Finn said. "I'll do another background check and bring him in for formal questioning. Maybe I can shake something loose."

"He's another sneaky one. He wasn't rattled when I quizzed him at the beach with Zandra."

"Finn! Oh, my goodness, Finn! Hurry!" Augustus raced over, his arms flapping and his face bright red.

"What is it?" Finn asked.

"The barn! It's on fire."

Chapter 16

Chargrilled surprise

"Stay back, everyone. The fire is under control, but the building isn't safe until the last of the flames have been extinguished," the local police chief, Chief Thomasina, gestured for the small group who had gathered to watch to remain at a safe distance as flames licked out of the roof of the storage barn.

Three firefighters directed a combination of high-pressure water hoses and magic over the barn, slowly extinguishing the flames. But it was too late to save the barn or the contents. The air was filled with a strong, acrid odor. It was a combination of burning hay and charred wood that had burned to a crisp as flames engulfed the building.

I stood with Finn. Zandra was beside me after I'd yanked on our bond to let her know there was trouble, her face glowing in the amber light. My throat felt scratchy after inhaling too much smoky air, so I insisted Zandra back away so she wouldn't suffer the same discomfort.

"Was there anyone in the barn when it caught fire?" she asked Finn.

He shook his head. "Everyone's been accounted for. Fortunately, there were no animals inside, either. It was a storage barn. We've lost the bulk of our feed supplies, though. We just had a new hay delivery, and that won't be cheap to replace."

"Better hay than lives," I said.

"That's something to be grateful for." Finn ran a hand through his hair. "I don't know how it got started. There was nothing in there to cause a spark. I'm always careful storing dry materials because of the fire risk, especially in hot conditions. But the weather hasn't been warm enough to cause something like this."

"We'll find the source of the fire once the blaze is put out." I studied the watching group. Dawn stood with Augustus, both of them looking stunned. There were a few of Finn's regular volunteers from town who dropped by once or twice a week to help. A few people from town had also arrived, having heard the news of the blaze and wanting to see if they could help or simply being nosy.

"We should check on the animals," Finn said. "The fire will have unsettled them, and it'll give me something to do other than watching helplessly and getting in the way."

"We'll help." I nudged Zandra with my head.

She nodded, and we followed Finn over to the other volunteers. Finn got everyone to work, checking each barn one by one and ensuring none of the residents had been startled by the fire or injured themselves if they'd panicked and tried to flee their stall or pen.

It took almost an hour to go around the barns, top up food and water, and say comforting words to everyone. By the time we were done, the flames were out, and the firefighters were packing their equipment, getting ready to leave.

I walked over to the fire chief with Finn and Zandra.

"There's not much left of the structure," he said to Finn. "Probably easiest if you pull the thing down and rebuild from scratch if you need it."

"I rent these barns, so I'll have to speak to the owner and see what they want to do," Finn said. "But I need all the buildings. I hope the landlord doesn't kick me out because this happened."

"It's not your fault," I said. Well, I secretly thought it could be Finn's fault, but now wasn't the time to lay blame. "Do you know what caused the fire?" I asked the fire chief.

"Not for certain. The blaze started in the back right corner. Whatever it was, it was an intense blast of heat. Did you store gas cans or chemicals in there? We didn't find any residue, but they don't always leave much behind if the heat is intense."

Finn tilted his head as he studied what was left of the barn. "It was mainly food for the animals."

"That's good, in a way. Chemicals explode. You could have had a much bigger mess on your hands if you stored gas or paint in there. I'll send my guy over tomorrow. He'll sweep the area and should be able to tell you what happened. And you'll need the information for the insurance."

Finn shook hands with the fire chief. "Thanks. I appreciate it."

He headed back to his team, and after a few minutes, the fire truck left the scene, along with most of the fire watchers from town, leaving a small group of volunteers behind.

We walked over to what was left of the barn. There was no roof, and two of the walls had partly collapsed. Inside, it was a black soggy mess. Nothing had been saved.

Finn blew out a breath and closed his eyes. "I need to get in touch with my suppliers to order new feed. Can't let the animals go hungry. And I need to contact the landowner. They won't be happy. They rented me these barns at a discounted rate because of what I use them for."

"These things happen," Zandra said. "Maybe it was a freak accident. Lightning?"

"Unfortunately, there's nothing freaky about this." I stood beside a small pile of charred dragon scales.

Finn walked over with Zandra and inspected them. He gulped, and his cheeks paled. "That's bad."

"Dragons did this deliberately?" Zandra asked.

"Is it any surprise?" I said to Finn. "You're hiding something precious from the dragons. They know you've got one of their babies. They've been lurking on the sidelines, trying to figure out your plan, but they're done waiting. And their warnings will get more extreme. If you're not careful, they'll burn this town to the ground looking for her. We can't allow that to happen."

Finn scrubbed a hand down his face. "Everything you're telling me is true, and the logical part of my brain understands that, but I still can't let her go.

My stomach hurts at the thought of not having her in my life."

"Then you're putting all of us at risk," Zandra said.

"Maybe... Maybe I could make a deal with the dragons. It's not my fault I bonded with the baby. She sang to me! She decided I should care for her," Finn said. "The dragons will understand. They'll want the best for the hatchling."

"The dragons will kill you!" I said. "They don't play around when one of their infants is taken."

"There must be a solution." Zandra blew out a breath. "A way to make everyone happy."

"The solution is to return her," I said.

Finn shook his head. "But she's so happy when she sees me. She'll cry if she has to leave."

Zandra rested a hand on Finn's shoulder. "This is tough for you, and we understand, but that dragon hatchling knows no different. She's never met another dragon. I hate to say it, but when she does, she won't care about you anymore."

"Are you sure? I'm impressive for an angel hybrid," Finn said, a sad smile crossing his face. "But I get it. I'm nothing to her. I was in the right place at the right time and was able to help her. I know I have to let her go, but I'm not sure I'm strong enough."

"You need to find the strength before the dragons make another move. Next time, they may direct their flames at you," I said.

"Hey! Is everyone okay?" Torrin jogged over, dressed in jeans and a plaid shirt. "I just heard about the fire. Otherwise, I'd have come to help."

"Thanks, buddy. The fire's out. No one was injured," Finn said.

Torrin nodded a greeting at us. "What started it?"

"These may provide the answer." I tapped a paw next to the dragon scales.

Torrin's eyes widened then a blank expression crossed his face. "What are they?"

"Don't play dumb with us."

He shrugged. "Do you have a lizard you're looking after at the sanctuary? Something with fire magic?"

I glared at Torrin and then Finn. They exchanged a glance, and Torrin discreetly shook his head. These two were hiding something, and it had to do with dragons. I wasn't happy about their concealment. If it only affected them, I wouldn't be concerned, but with the dragons stepping up their interest in this place, it left us vulnerable. And when my wonderful witch was vulnerable, I got mean.

"I've got things to do," Finn said. "There's been smoke damage to the office and to the volunteer accommodation. I must find an alternative place for them to stay until it's cleaned up. I can let them stay in another barn, but it'll be basic and needs work before I can let them move in."

"I'll look at the damaged barn, see if there's anything that can be salvaged." Torrin strode off.

"Finn, wait a moment," I said. "Does Torrin know about your hatchling?"

He hesitated. "Why would he know anything about her?"

"Because he has connections in that community," I said. "We wondered if he was helping you negotiate a deal to keep the hatchling."

Finn gently smiled. "Nice idea, but Torrin's not a negotiator. Well, unless you count him using his fists to get what he wants. Are you helping or not?"

I jumped onto Zandra's shoulder, and we lagged behind Finn as he walked over to his volunteers. I pressed my booping snooter against her ear. "They're hiding something, and we need to get to the bottom of it. The dragons are heating things up, and it's only a matter of time before this gets out of hand."

"A barn burned to the ground isn't considered getting out of hand?"

"That's an appetizer for most dragons. I fear worse is to come if we don't get control of Finn and his dragon situation."

"Zandra, can you help Dawn move her things?" Finn asked as we joined the small group.

"There's no need." Dawn glared at me. "I can do it on my own. I don't have much stuff."

"Then it won't take long for us to assist you," I said. "Lead the way."

Dawn's eyes narrowed. "Finn, do you work with this cat?"

He glanced over and nodded. "Sometimes. Is there a problem?"

"Oh! It's just that... I thought... Never mind. Follow me. You already know the way." Dawn turned and stomped off.

"Someone doesn't like you," Zandra muttered.

"Because I know her secret," I said. "At least part of it."

Dawn had been accurate when she said she didn't have much stuff. She filled three boxes with belongings and stuffed her backpack full of clothes until it bulged. It took less than twenty minutes to gather her worldly goods. In that time, she barely spoke to us.

While Dawn had her back turned, sealing boxes, I snuck to her backpack. Zandra knew what I was doing, so she engaged Dawn in conversation. I poked around in the pockets until I found Dawn's little black book full of enigmatic initials and sums of money. I pulled it out and tucked it under the rug.

"That's everything." Dawn stepped back and looked around the room. "The smoke damage isn't bad. I'd be okay to stay here. I've stayed in a lot worse places. At least this place feels safe."

"The smell could make you sick," Zandra said. "My throat hurts after breathing in the smoky air. Finn's doing the right thing by moving you, and he'll make sure everything is cleaned up fast. You'll be back here within a week."

I nodded along, silently wondering if Dawn would be back at all. She was secretive, and although she had an alibi for Hortense's murder, she was hiding things. Things that weren't legal if the amount of money it made her was anything to go by.

By the time everyone had moved and we'd done a final check on the animals, it was close to midnight, and my witch was tiring. Although I was intrigued to delve into the mysteries in Dawn's notebook, we'd tackle it in the morning. A close encounter with a dragon meant we needed food, a shower, rest, and recharge before the investigation continued.

Chapter 17
Unwelcome clues

Zandra's mobile snow globe buzzing by the side of the bed woke us the next morning. It was early, just past six, and I'd hoped for a couple more hours of sleep before rolling out of bed to go to work.

Zandra made a grunting, snort-like noise and flopped onto her side, ignoring the buzzing.

I clambered over her and checked the mobile snow globe. "It's a message from Finn. It could be important."

There was more grumbling and muttered words of a less-than-pure nature before Zandra fumbled around and lifted the offending item. She flipped onto her back and stared at it, blinking slowly. "It's from Finn."

"I told you that." I wriggled up until I was beside her head and sniffed her warm ear.

She grunted. "A film crew is going to the sanctuary. Celeste heard about the fire, and she wants to help him raise funds to rebuild the barn by doing a fundraiser."

"That's generous of her," I said. "I wonder if our unfriendly camera guy, Percival, will be there? It would be the perfect opportunity to grill him and ask why he lied about his alibi. Maybe get him to slip up and reveal what happened between him and Hortense the night she died."

"Good plan. We'll have to let Barney know we'll be in late," Zandra replied. "Work's quiet, though, so he won't mind."

"We'll tell him we're helping Finn after the fire. He may be there himself, lending a hand. You know Barney: animals first." I wriggled onto the pillow. "And it would be good to check in and make sure everything's okay with Finn and he's had no more dragon warnings overnight."

I sat on the end of the bed while Zandra rolled out, stretched, and headed to the bathroom. "We need to get him to see sense about his new baby." She kept the door open so we could talk.

"Whatever he's up to, it involves Torrin, so that could mean bad news."

"Torrin's not so bad," she said. "He just lets his feral dragon side out more often than others are comfortable with."

"It's the feral dragon side that's got me worried. What if he wants to keep the hatchling, too?"

"You think they want to raise her together?"

I chuckled. "They'd make an adorable blended family."

Zandra came out of the bathroom. "We'll have to have tough conversations with Finn if he doesn't get his act together."

"It will be uncomfortable, but he'll understand we're trying to help."

Zandra walked over and sat on the side of the bed as she put on her socks. "What about this?" She lifted Dawn's notebook and tossed it onto the bed.

I'd retrieved it after Dawn had moved and given it to Zandra for safe keeping. "Dawn's a puzzle. She's not involved in the murder, but she's up to something. I have a bad feeling it's something illegal. I don't want her exploiting Finn."

"Why do the scribbles in that notebook mean she's exploiting Finn?"

"I've yet to figure that out, which is why I took it. We need to decipher the clues and see where they lead us."

"But first, we confront our prime suspect in this murder investigation," Zandra said. "We've caught Percival in a lie, but it's not enough to charge him with murder."

"Then let's go rattle his cage and see if we can get that smug veneer to slip."

After breakfast, dropping by animal control to let Barney know we'd be late getting started, and messaging Finn to tell him we were on our way and what our plan was, we headed to the sanctuary in Zandra's van.

The air still had a smoke-tinged tang as we parked and walked around. The damaged barn looked much worse in the daylight, with its wet side sagging and its contents blackened and soaked.

Finn bounded over with a smile on his face. "Can you believe it? As soon as Celeste heard about the fire, she contacted me and said she wanted to help. I'm one lucky guy."

"It's great news," Zandra said.

"The camera crew is getting here in twenty minutes. They'll film the damage, interview me and some volunteers, and then take shots of the animals. Celeste wants to tug on people's heartstrings so they open their purses and give more. I've promised her lots of sad, fluffy faces."

"She sounds like a wonderful patron," I said. "If you need me to play sad cat, just say the word."

"Celeste said her company does this all the time for the communities they have a presence in. You always hear big business say they help local communities, so I'm thrilled she was so quick to help."

"And you've put on your whitest shirt for the cameras. It makes your teeth gleam," I said.

He chuckled. "I figured angel charm would do no harm. Or should I go for the smoke-damaged and sad-eyed look?"

"It could secure you more funds. If they think you've been working hard all night, saving the unwanted animals in the community, you'll look like a warrior angel fighting for the voiceless."

"Yeah, good point. I'll go smear myself with dirt."

While Finn went off to make himself look suitably disheveled, a van rolled into the sanctuary. Percival climbed out, followed by his assistant Max and the presenter, Cheri. They huddled together for a couple of minutes, talking and pointing at the barn until Cheri spotted Finn and hurried over to join him.

We walked over to Percival, who was unloading equipment from the back of the van.

"Greetings. Back for more filming?" I asked.

"What gave it away?" Percival replied, his back still turned to us.

Zandra looked at me and rolled her eyes. "Not a morning person, huh?"

"You could say that." Percival turned. "Oh! You two."

I twitched my ears. "Back again."

"You're still poking around that murder? Or are you figuring out what happened to this place?"

"Both." I paused, waiting for Finn to join us. "We were about to reveal to Percival that his alibi didn't check out."

Finn nodded, his expression serious. "You told us you were talking to Cheri, but she has no recollection of that conversation."

Percival looked momentarily stunned. "She's lying! She's easy on the eye but doesn't have a brain cell to spare. And the woman wears so much perfume, the fumes make her high. She forgot we were together. I can remind her if you like."

"No need. You didn't tell us the truth," I said.

"I'm not the one with the problem." Percival jabbed a finger at me. "Maybe Cheri's got something to hide. Have you thought she could be the killer? Don't trust her. Did you know she's married while making goo-goo eyes at me?"

"We found out. She was open with us when we spoke to her. We also found out Cheri isn't interested in you. You lied about that too."

"Did I?" Percival smirked. "Or was she covering her back because she doesn't want to be found out as a cheater? Cheri's into me. I'm irresistible."

"We could bring her into this conversation and ask her." I inhaled to call Cheri over from her inspection of the barn.

"No! Don't do that. I... I don't want to embarrass her. Cheri may be as thick as a plank of wood, but there's no malice in her. I don't want her getting upset. She's such an ugly crier. Puts you right off."

"How chivalrous of you," I said.

Percival shrugged. "We were having a bit of fun that night. Flirting and fooling around, but it was nothing serious. I dunno. Maybe I read too much into things. I could have misremembered her saying she likes me."

"Did you also misremember your alibi for the time of Hortense's murder?" I asked.

He growled out a breath. "It wasn't me! Go hassle the woman who runs the bakery and that dangerous big cat who's always following her around. Hortense hated her. And I saw them arguing!"

"It wasn't them," I said.

"Do you know for sure?"

"We do," Finn said. "Tia and Binky are no longer suspects."

"Well, I saw Hortense arguing with other people here, too. I even filmed it." Percival was sweating.

"Hortense argued with everyone," I said.

"So why pick on me? If everybody hated her, you've got plenty of suspects. I'm not from around here. I didn't know her."

"You believe Hortense stole your equipment, though," Finn said. "And we know she damaged some of it when she threw it on the ground."

"That's motive for murder?" Percival shook his head. "I wouldn't kill anyone over a damaged kit."

"Even though it was expensive?" I asked.

"It can be replaced." Percival stopped sorting through his equipment, and a serious expression crossed his face. "I didn't do it. And I can prove it to you."

I licked a paw and washed an ear. "With your actual alibi this time?"

"Yeah, whatever. But I'll show you you're wrong. Then you'll owe me an apology. My lazy assistant, Max, was supposed to have edited the footage from the night of the bakery opening. He only did half of it, so the later stuff is still raw footage. I shot that. I was behind the camera all the time."

"How does that prove your innocence?" I asked.

"Because of the insanely strong magic around this place." Percival scowled at nothing in particular. "These magical towns are a nightmare to film in because of equipment glitches. I've got wards around the camera, and they're supposed to be guaranteed free from magical interference, but they never work properly when they're around a lot of magic. Ever since coming to Crimson Cove, the power circuits keep overloading. It's given me a headache and extra work I could do without."

"We're not making apologies for being supremely powerful beings," I said.

Percival grunted at me. "Anyway, there's footage of me here that evening. I had to keep setting the camera on a tripod and fiddling with the settings so it didn't overheat or malfunction. You can see me in and out of shot plenty of times. And when I'm doing a montage, I talk out loud and make voice notes about how I want to frame the shots. You can hear me on the camera too. I did that all evening until only thirty seconds before Hortense was found. It was my bad luck I'd put down the camera to grab food when I heard the scream. I missed the best bit."

I hissed softly. What an odious individual.

"I'd like to see that footage," Finn said.

"I can show you now."

We gathered around Percival's camera, which had a flip-out screen so we could watch the recording. He took a few minutes to set up and then pressed play.

"The camera is time and date stamped, and there's no way it can be manipulated on the raw footage. You can do it in post editing, but you'll see all this stuff is untouched. I keep coming in and out of shots, and you'll hear me talking. The final edit will have that erased."

We watched several minutes of footage. Percival kept speeding through it and showing us where he was. After another ten minutes of watching, we were convinced. Unfortunately, Percival wasn't the killer.

"Does that mean I'm in the clear? You won't keep hassling me?" Percival set down his camera.

"I believe so," Finn said. "I don't suppose your footage showed Hortense fighting with anyone that evening?"

"No, she hated being on camera. Every time I thought she was coming to complain, I swung the camera in her face, and she scuttled away." He laughed to himself. "And as for my stolen equipment, I suspected Hortense had taken it out of spite, so I didn't like her, but it turns out it wasn't her."

"Someone else took your equipment?" I asked.

Percival rubbed the back of his neck and looked a little shamefaced. "I left it in a barn that night. With everything that went on, I forgot about it. I snuck back and picked it up then told Cheri that Max had stored it in the wrong place so I didn't get the blame."

I was almost sorry Percival wasn't guilty of murder. The world would be a better place without this hideous individual in it.

"And I did speak to Cheri that evening, but she must have forgotten. It was a busy night. Now, I need to get on with filming. We want to get your appeal aired today before the fire becomes old news." Percival lifted the camera onto his shoulder and walked to the barn.

Finn blew out a breath. "Our prime suspect is in the clear. Where does that leave us?"

"Returning to the start and figuring out what clue we missed," I said.

"And as much as we'd love to do that right now, we need to get to work," Zandra said. "Are you okay if we go, Finn?"

He nodded. "Sure. I'll be here for a while helping with the appeal. Cythera knows where I am. But I'm stumped! And I have no clue what to tell Cythera. This investigation has hit a dead end."

"One thing we don't want her to do is look at the original suspects too hard. When Cythera gets backed into a corner, she makes mistakes," I said. "And if she goes after Tia and Binky again, she'll get more than a warning nip this time if Binky gets angry."

After leaving the sanctuary, we headed back to town. Zandra pulled a small bag out of the passenger well as she climbed out.

"What have you got in there?" I asked. "Snacks?"

"Nothing special. A change of clothes and cosmetics. Let's get inside and see what fun jobs Barney has for us today. Maybe he'll send us after those funky-smelling toads again. I'm sure those things have been hexed with something gross."

I hurried along beside her. "For what reason?"

"The bag?" Zandra's stride increased.

I kept up with her. "Yes! Why bring a change of clothes and cosmetics with you? You have some in your locker."

She pulled open the door. "Well... I'm meeting Randal for lunch."

Chapter 18

Breakthrough

"How is this a good idea?" Sage's nose was pressed against the glass of the pizza parlor.

I sat next to her, and Binky sat on my other side.

"When you said we were going on a lunch date, I didn't expect this," Binky said. "I was thinking steak and gossip about the murder."

"I need to make sure they get it right." My gaze was fixed on Zandra and Randal. They'd just sat down at a table for two and were ordering from the menu. "Zandra can't give up on love, and if things go awry, I must be around to set them back on the correct path."

"To interfere, you mean. How do you know they have a correct path?" Sage asked. "Why can't Zandra be happy on her own?"

"She'll never be on her own because she has me, but she needs love that I can't give her."

"And you think Randal can?" Binky asked. "I like him, but he's nervy, and Zandra's a whole lotta witch. Maybe too much for him."

"Zandra sees something in Randal, and I want to make her happy. And I trust him. He's a genuinely nice guy, and he adores my witch. Randal will treat her well."

"You make her happy," Sage said. "Vorana's been single forever, and you don't see her miserable. That's because she has me."

I glanced at my surly friend. "Have you ever asked Vorana if she'd like a companion that doesn't come with fur and a tail?"

Sage grunted. "I'm enough of a companion for her. Why complicate something that works?"

"To make our witches even happier," I said. "Look! They must have ordered."

"I wonder what they got." Binky purred softly to herself. "Something with lots of meat? I keep asking for a pizza with a meat crust, but Tia says that's basically a steak with toppings."

"Mmmmm. That sounds amazing," Sage said. "I'm hungry. Steak pizza with extra cheese would be amazing."

"I'll treat you to pizza after this," I said.

Sage's fur bristled, her head turned, and she hissed.

I remained focused on Zandra. Sage was probably reacting to seeing a tree rat. "What's the matter?"

"That sneaky little turncoat is here. How dare he!"

I risked a glance away from the window. Barney was on the other side of the street. Ember Dreamscape was with him and had a magical leash attached to him. The restraints glowed on his throat and chest, but he was trotting along happily, chatting with Barney as if they were the best of friends.

"Remember, I told you he's back in town for rehab?" I said to Sage as she continued hissing. "Barney thinks he can help Ember."

"The only help that devious cat needs is a boot up the backside on his way out of town. Nobody wants him here." Sage shimmered with magic.

"Easy, now. Sammy thinks Ember has turned a corner. He says he's doing well."

"Ember's a scheming liar!" Sage said. "He almost killed our witches."

We watched until they were out of sight. Sage kept growling until I stilled her with a calming paw.

"Any news on when Sammy's getting out?" Binky asked me.

"Not yet, but if his rehab continues to go well, Sammy and Tinkerbell may get long community service and not serve any time in prison. It'll involve years of giving back to the community they almost destroyed, but I'm encouraging him to take the deal. And the werewolves have spoken up in Sammy's defense, which convinced Angel Force he wasn't acting under his own free will when he went rogue. I'm hopeful for a positive outcome."

"Is that a good thing?" Sage said. "After everything Sammy went through, there'll be scars. He's not the same cat I knew. He has a darker edge. He could be unstable. Maybe prison is the best place for him."

I turned back and made sure everything was going well with Zandra and Randal. "I'm hopeful for his future. And maybe ours too."

Sage twitched an ear. "You want him back?"

"I'm considering it. There's still something between us."

We settled in and watched Zandra and Randal for ten minutes. Zandra had passed something to Randal, and although I couldn't see what it was, it must have intrigued him because he spent a few minutes flicking back and forth through the pages, writing things down on his napkin.

"That doesn't look overly romantic," Sage said. "Randal is ignoring Zandra."

"Maybe he's writing her a poem," Binky said. "That's romantic."

I tensed as Randal leapt from his seat, knocking his chair over. He gestured at whatever he'd been writing and then at Zandra.

"Something's wrong!" I needed to fix this before their date veered into disastrous territory. I dashed to the door, but before I got inside the pizza parlor, Randal and Zandra were already leaving.

Zandra looked down at me and sighed. "What a surprise to see you here."

"What's going on? You can't be leaving so soon."

"We have to. Randal's had a breakthrough in the murder investigation."

I waved a quick goodbye to Sage and Binky, ignoring their complaints that I'd promised them pizza. "What did he find out?"

"I brought Dawn's notebook with me. Randal's great with puzzles, so I thought he could figure out what the initials mean."

"That's not romantic date material!" I hurried along with her as we followed Randal. "What did he learn?"

Randal was way ahead of us, marching like an Olympic speed-walker, the notepad clutched in his hands.

"He figured out what the initials mean. Randal! Wait up." Zandra lifted me onto her shoulder and broke into an uncharacteristic jog.

He slowed briefly but still continued at a quick pace.

"Tell Juno what you told me," Zandra said as we reached him.

He nodded at me. "The initials in the notepad relate to animal names. See here. HB is horned bat. FTW is fanged tiger worm. And 8TB is an eight-toed babboa."

"Randal thinks the sums of money next to them are the payments Dawn received for locating these animals for someone," Zandra said.

Shock spiked through me. "Dawn loves animals. Why is she selling them?"

"Look at the sums of money involved," Randal said. "You could live comfortably on that amount."

"The bundle of cash in her backpack! That's where it came from."

"And Dawn's volunteer role at Finn's animal sanctuary is the perfect cover," Zandra said. "She has daily access to all kinds of animals."

"Someone would notice animals going missing," I said. "How is she able to do it?"

"That's what we need to find out."

"And we need to find out who she's been selling them to." I slowed. "What if it was Hortense? This gives us a whole new motive for murder." I mulled over the possibilities as we raced to Angel Force.

Finn was sitting at his desk but stood as we came in. "What's up?"

Randal rapidly explained his findings, and a stunned Finn pulled up the case files, rechecking the suspects' financials to see if there was a connection to the amounts of money Dawn was paid and the recordings in her notebook.

"Look at this," Finn said. "This is Hortense's financial information."

I sat on the desk next to his computer and peered at the screen.

"These amounts tie to the sums Dawn has in her notebook." Finn raked a hand through his hair. "I can't believe it. Dawn fooled me. I thought she was an animal lover. She takes amazing care of them, and she's always around when any of them need soothing. But she was volunteering so she could take them and sell them to Hortense."

"How has Dawn gotten away with it?" Zandra said to Finn. "You must keep records of your residents."

"Of course! But I recognize these initials. When the animals are ready to leave the sanctuary, they need to be transported. That's usually a task for volunteers. The last time I asked, Dawn stepped forward. She was supposed to take them to their new forever homes." Finn closed his eyes and massaged his forehead. "None of them made it. She drove them to wherever Hortense wanted them and left them. I don't feel so good."

"Put your head between your knees. You've had a shock," I said.

"This news makes my sanctuary a laughingstock. Dawn's undone all of my hard work."

"You've saved many lives." I jumped on Finn's back as he leaned forward, taking deep breaths. "Your sanctuary is marvelous. Don't let one rotten apple ruin things. No one will blame you for this."

"We may be able to get them back," Zandra said. "Hortense wanted to buy Tia's bakery to open some kind of exotic animal store, so she must be housing them somewhere."

My stomach flipped, and I gently kneaded Finn's shoulders. "I believe Hortense actually wanted to open an exotic animal pelt store."

Finn groaned. "Don't say that. If she hurt any of those animals, I'm not sure I'll be able to control myself."

"If you need to go full demon and take your anger out on Dawn, we won't stop you," I said.

Zandra gently cleared her throat. "We will, but we understand why you're upset."

Finn drew in a deep breath, waited for me to hop off his back, and then he stood. "Dawn's got the perfect motive for killing Hortense."

"She may have wanted to stop trading," I said, "but Hortense wouldn't let her. Dawn got desperate, so she murdered her."

"I think the murder has more to do with money," Randal said. "Look at the payments. They started high, but the last few have been half the original amount for the same animal."

"Hortense started paying Dawn less," I said, "and of course, she couldn't complain because that would reveal what she was doing. So, she got her revenge."

A flicker of red demon energy sparked across Finn's wings, making us all take a step back. He lifted a hand. "I'm in control. I won't lose focus. Not when I have an arrest to make."

"We'll come with you," I said.

After letting Barney know we'd be late back because of an animal-related emergency, we were out the door of Angel Force.

"Won't Cythera want to be involved in this arrest?" I asked.

"She's out again with Maverick. He's being demanding with their wedding plans. It's trying her patience, but so far, she's gritting her teeth and smiling through it all. Cythera won't mind me taking the lead on this. She knows how important the animal sanctuary is to me."

"I know you're angry with Dawn, and you have every right to be," I said, "but go easy on her, or she'll panic and run."

"If she does, I'll chase her down and make sure she goes nowhere. No one messes with my sanctuary. I've been such an idiot. Too trusting."

"Perfectly trusting," I said.

He glanced at the sky. "I'll fly there."

"We'll magic our way over," I said. "See you in a few seconds."

"I wish I could help, but I need to get back to work," Randal said.

Zandra turned to him, and an awkward smile twisted her mouth. "It was a good date for the first fifteen minutes. And I should thank you. You figured out who the killer is."

He smiled and blushed. "I got lucky. If I wasn't a puzzle geek, I'd have never figured it out. Third time's a charm for another date?"

"I'll think about it," Zandra said.

"I hate to interrupt this romantic moment, but we need to move," I said. "I don't want Finn confronting Dawn alone. Not while his demon side is so close to the surface."

"Of course. Go! I'll see you at work," Randal said.

I hopped on Zandra's shoulder, not missing Randal's regretful expression, cast a translocation spell around us, and we appeared at the sanctuary just as Finn touched down. It only took a moment to find Dawn. She was carrying an empty animal cage, which she set down as we approached her.

"Is something wrong?" Unease flickered across her face. "Finn, you look angry. Did I do something I shouldn't?"

"Explain this." He held out the black notepad. "Dawn, how could you?"

Her eyes widened, and she tensed. "What's that?"

"Evidence of the illegal deals you've made with the animals from this sanctuary. The animals you were supposed to protect! Rescued animals! Animals we were entrusted with to give a better life. Dawn, you broke my trust." Finn's breath heaved out of him as he struggled to control his emotions.

Dawn's gaze flickered over us, then she turned and ran, whacking into the cage she'd put down. She hit the dirt but rolled to her feet and fled.

Finn's hands clenched, and he shot into the air. He zoomed over Dawn's head and thudded down in front of her. "You're going nowhere until I get an explanation for this soulless behavior."

She skidded to a halt and backed away from him. "I... I can explain."

We followed but stayed silent, letting Finn do the talking.

"I thought you cared for these animals," Finn said.

"I do! I love volunteering here. I've never been happier."

"You've been selling them! Selling them to Hortense."

She gasped. "You don't know who I've been selling to. There are no details in the notepad."

"Unfortunately, you're not that clever," I said. "You may have only kept handwritten notes of your transactions, but Hortense withdrew the money to pay you from her own account. The exact amount paid for each animal."

"And when Hortense started paying you less, you killed her," Finn said.

Dawn's hand flew to her face. "No! I didn't kill her. I already told you I didn't do it. You know that!"

"But you sold the sanctuary animals to her?" Finn said. "The animals I entrusted to your care to go to their loving, forever homes, where they should have been happy and safe, no longer scared. You really did that?"

Dawn's shoulders sagged. "I... I had to. I needed the money."

"What for? You should have asked me for money if you were struggling," Finn said. "I value you as a volunteer. We could have worked something out.

You already get free room and board here. What were you having problems with?"

"You don't understand. I need a lot of money, and fast." Dawn's hands trembled. "I'm... I'm in debt. A lot of debt to an awful man. A vicious, violent man, who won't have any problem killing me if I don't give it back to him by the end of the month. I thought I could outrun him and lay low here. But somehow, he found me. He threatened me and said no one would come looking for me when I disappeared. I was terrified."

"And desperate enough to sell the things you love to Hortense to clear your debt." I stepped in front of Dawn deliberately, so I was in Finn's path if he lost control.

There were tears in her eyes as she nodded. "I was on track to make the money back, but then Hortense halved her payments. I begged her not to, but she laughed at me. She said if I had a problem, to complain to Angel Force. She had me over a barrel, and she knew it. But I promise you, I didn't kill her. I wanted to, but I didn't."

"You're coming with me," Finn said. "We're charging you with Hortense's murder."

"No! Ask Augustus. He's my alibi."

"I've heard enough. Let's move." Finn caught hold of Dawn's shoulder, and she didn't protest as he flew off with her back to Angel Force.

"So, that's it?" Zandra asked after we'd stood in silence for a few seconds. "I can handle my lunch date being ruined if we caught the killer."

I sat back and watched Finn and Dawn disappear. "There's just one problem. Dawn still has an alibi."

Chapter 19

Unreliable witness

We'd had to return to work after Finn took Dawn to Angel Force, and I could do nothing but hope Finn kept control of himself. He was devastated by the discovery she'd betrayed him and sent some of the animals he cared about so deeply into a terrifying situation.

Zandra tossed down her pen and sighed. "I can't concentrate. I keep worrying about what's going on."

"Me too. We could visit Angel Force and see how things have progressed."

"We can only push our luck so far with Barney."

"He'll understand if we need to step out for half an hour. This case is about exploited animals as well as murder. He'll only want the best outcome in this situation."

Zandra tugged on the end of her hair. "You're worrying Finn will do something crazy, too?"

"He was putting on a good front when he took Dawn away, but he was angry as well as upset. And when Finn gets angry..."

"The world turns red, and he goes all evil demon on us." She glared at her paperwork. "I've still got three reports to finish. You go. Get an update from Angel Force and then report back. By now, Dawn should have confessed, and this'll be over. She should be safely behind bars where no one can get to her. Finn included."

I didn't need to be told twice and dashed away from animal control and over to Angel Force. I discovered Finn in the kitchen, making himself a strong coffee and muttering. His wings were at half mast, showing his frustration.

He looked up as I approached. There was sadness in his smile.

"Any news?" I hopped onto the kitchen counter since Cythera wasn't around to tell me off and complain that it wasn't hygienic.

"Nothing good. Dawn is still saying she's innocent of murder. She's willing to admit to the crime of selling animals on the black market to Hortense, but that's it."

"Has Dawn told you where the animals were taken?"

"She doesn't know. Or at least that's what she's claiming. Dawn met Hortense at the same drop-off point two miles outside of Crimson Cove, and they'd move the animals into another van. Then Hortense would leave."

I let out a soft sigh of concern. "Now Hortense is dead, and those animals are trapped somewhere."

"It's all I can think about! I want to shake the information out of Dawn, but if she doesn't have it..."

"And then there's the problem of her alibi," I said.

Finn grimaced. "Dawn is insisting Augustus was with her when Hortense was killed. She only walked away from him for a moment because she saw a light on in the storage barn, and no one was supposed to be in there."

"And you've checked with Augustus?"

"I got in touch with him, and he confirmed he was with Dawn. He was insistent she wasn't involved. I asked him about the animals, and he seemed surprised. He said he knew nothing about it, and if he had, he'd have told me straight away."

"When Augustus started as a volunteer, you said you had trouble getting all of his references."

"Sure. One checked out, but I never heard from the other one. Why do you ask?"

"Do you still have their information? I should visit them face to face and make sure he's not been keeping anything from us."

"You're welcome to give it a shot, but you won't get anything if his referee is still at the silent retreat."

"For so long? Surely, he'd be home by now."

"It might have been a silent order. Augustus said the guy worked there sometimes." Finn pinched the bridge of his nose. "I'll have to check my records."

"Maybe a silent order would bend the rules and let me speak to him if they know how serious this is," I said.

Finn scrubbed at his chin. "You're thinking Augustus could be in on this too?"

"There must be a reason he's prepared to give Dawn an alibi. Maybe she's got something on him and is forcing him to lie for her. Until we get her confession that she did it or we expose her alibi as fabricated, you're stuck."

"As Cythera made me well aware. She's given me twenty-four hours to make the murder charge stick or I have to release Dawn. I'll grab the details."

I waited in the kitchen, investigating the angel's snacks left unattended on the counter until Finn returned. "Here are Augustus's referees. I had them in my contacts. Are you going alone?"

"Zandra's stuck at work. I'll be fine. I'll be there and back before you know it. And hopefully with good news."

"Anything you can do to help is welcome. Every time I think we get a breakthrough in this case, something blocks it, and it becomes more complicated." He thumped down his coffee mug.

"And you're struggling to focus because you want to break heads and protect your animals."

"I have to know what happened to them. I feel like a fraud. I'm supposed to protect them, and I was letting the volunteers sell them right under my nose."

"We'll fix this, my feathered friend. Don't obliterate anyone whilst I'm gone." I patted his hand with my paw as I memorized the details. Then, I cast a translocation spell and arrived at my first destination.

Eldermoor nestled amidst rolling hills. A once pretty town, most of the streets were a flicker of their former selves, and in the run-down district of Shadowvale lay the silent retreat where Augustus's referee was supposed to work. The building looked abandoned, its once-majestic façade marred by time, the bricks weathered and cracked, revealing glimpses of the enchantment that once imbued them. Moss and ivy crawled up the decaying walls, casting eerie shadows upon its weather-beaten face.

There was a "keep out" notice on the front door, faded by the weather and scrawled with graffiti, and after I'd walked around the building twice, checking for signs of magical concealment, I realized this place hadn't been lived in for a long time, and there was nothing magical left.

"Is there a problem?" A woman from the nail bar next to the crumbling building stood on the step, her hands on her hips.

"Greetings. No problem. I'm seeking the Order of the Magical Mages. They're a silent order. I have this as their address."

It looked like she tried to frown, but her forehead appeared frozen. "Silent order? Like monks?"

"No, magical mages. Have they moved on?"

"I've been here ten years, and no one's used that building during that time. You've got the wrong place."

"You've never heard of the Order of the Magical Mages?"

"Can't help you." She flashed me a startling white smile. "I can give you a discount on claw glitter, though. Thirty percent off if you're a walk-in."

"I appreciate the offer, but I'm working." I flashed her a polite cat smile.

She flashed sparkly talons back at me, the tips of her nails a glossy green. "Your loss."

I walked both sides of the street, attempting to find anything related to the Order of the Magical Mages, but there was no sign of them. The area had a downtrodden and neglected feel, most of the stores drooping with despair or already empty, having given up the battle against neglect.

Augustus hadn't been truthful about this reference. What else had he lied about?

I magicked myself to the next address. It was listed as an apartment above a bar in Katkin Mallow. The name was prettier than the destination. The bar was in full swing, with loud music blaring out the door and magical smoke drifting in the breeze, tinging the air with cheap musk and the hint of salacious fun.

I entered to discover a throng of sweaty bodies, the scent of alcohol heavy in the air. I weaved through, careful not to get my paws trodden on, and hopped onto the bar.

It took several minutes of paw waving before the female bartender strode over. "What can I do you for, cutie? First time?" Her smile was all gold teeth.

"Greetings. I'm looking for Donnie Washington."

"What do you want with that lowlife?" Her nose wrinkled.

"Information. Is he here?"

"I saw him skulk in about half an hour ago. I've yet to throw him out."

"Doesn't he live in the apartment upstairs?"

"Live here!" She snorted. "I live upstairs. Donnie the Donut's been banned. Banned from most places around here because he can't keep his hands to himself."

I reared back. "He's a molester?"

"No, sweetie. He's a pickpocket. I've been keeping an eye on him, making sure he doesn't mess with my regulars. My advice is to stay out of his way. That loser will only bring trouble to your door." She waved away a customer who held out an empty glass. "Sure, he's got charm and a hot smile when he wants something, but when your back's turned, his hands are in your purse, and he's running off with your worldly goods."

"If you'd allow me to, once I've spoken to him, I'll happily escort him off the premises." I glimmered magic around me. "My favor to you for being so helpful."

She chuckled. "I like you. If you think you can take him on, be my guest. He's dressed head to toe in black, has a dyed black goatee, and he's wearing a baseball cap. His jacket has a wolf motif on the back in black and red stitching. He says he likes to move with the shadows, so he dresses like one. Such an idiot."

I thanked her and remained on the bar, scanning the crowd. It took me several minutes, but I picked out Donnie. He was lifting a wallet from the back of someone's jeans. He pocketed it and moved on. I tracked him, stepping over drinks left on the bar. He headed into a shadowed corner, pulled out the wallet, and flicked through the contents.

I coiled, leapt over people's heads, aided by a dash of magic, and landed next to him.

Donnie jumped up from his seat, his hand going to his heart. "Why'd you do that? I nearly died of fright when you landed. Get out of here."

I ignored his waving hand. "Greetings! Sit down, Donnie. We need to talk."

"I'm not..." He slumped back into his seat as I whacked him with a spell.

"Let's be polite. There's no need to cause trouble. And I'm sure you don't want me to alert the bartender that you're up to your old tricks." I looked at the wallet.

Donnie glowered at me as he rubbed his chest. "What do you want?"

"Information about Augustus Dray."

He pushed back his baseball cap. He was a young guy, no more than thirty, with narrow eyes and a long nose. "What's he done this time?"

"Why don't you tell me how you know him?"

"Same as I know most people. We met in prison."

"Augustus served time?"

Donnie grinned. "He wasn't called Augustus when we met. He made up that identity when he got out. He wanted a clean start and for no one to know him. Last I heard, he was moving around, working here or there, telling everyone he was some nature wizard who communes with animals. I lost interest at that point. The guy talks nonsense."

"Augustus was inside for stealing, just like you?"

He tucked the stolen wallet into his inside jacket pocket. "Maybe. What's it to you? And who are you? Why all the questions?"

"I'm Juno. And I work with Angel Force. No! There's no need to run, and there's no point in running. I'll chase you, and this'll become much less pleasant. I need information, and then I'll be on my way. I have zero interest in your pilfering activities."

Donnie looked suspicious as he remained in his seat. "I can't help. I've lost touch with Augustus. When I knew him, he was Alfie Dragnet. He thought he could change and start over, but once you're caught in this cycle, you can never change. No one wants to give you a second chance. And some habits die hard." He patted the lump where the wallet sat.

"Augustus had you listed as one of his referees for an animal sanctuary he volunteers at."

Donnie relaxed back into his seat, a smirk on his face. "Not just one of them. He wanted me to be a former employer and a weird magical mage who went into some silent order so I couldn't be contacted."

"You didn't mind taking part in the deception?"

"Augustus said it was something to do with animals, so I didn't think there'd be a problem. And he said he'd pay me, so I agreed. I have several mobile snow globes as part of my business empire, so he made up two names for me to use when I got the call, and I gave him two of my numbers."

"Yet you didn't follow through," I said. "Why was that?"

"I got a call from some guy called Finn and did what I was supposed to do. I pretended I'd hired Augustus, and he was a good guy. Finn then got in touch with the magical mage. He left a message, and I was going to reply, but then I remembered Augustus never paid me! The money never came through. I shouldn't have been surprised. He was never a man of his word."

I nodded as I digested this information. Augustus was a criminal, had no reliable references, and was associating with Dawn, who'd broken some serious laws. Were they in on it together? Dawn was tiny, so maybe she needed someone to hold Hortense while she killed her. They could have provided alibis for each other to cover their guilt.

"Are we done? I have pockets to pick."

"Thank you for your time. You've been helpful."

"You haven't. You answered none of my questions," Donnie said. "What's Augustus got himself messed up in? Stolen something he shouldn't?"

I hopped down. "Nothing so trivial. He's involved in a murder."

Chapter 20

Lies unravel

"Is there anyone who isn't lying to me?" Finn paced the length of the kitchen in Angel Force, visibly agitated after I'd updated him about Augustus.

Zandra was also there, having joined us after finishing work at animal control.

"We need to speak to Augustus again," I said. "He could be covering for Dawn or even involved in the murder."

"Maybe they both did it," Zandra said. "Dawn got Hortense with the hayfork and Augustus choked her with the pasty."

"Let me check if Augustus's real details have come through the system yet." Finn stomped out of the room.

"I haven't seen him this angry for a long time," Zandra said, lifting me onto her shoulder before following Finn.

Squinting at the screen and scowling, Finn said, "Here he is. Alfie Freakin' Dragnet. Long history of theft going back five years."

"Any incidents of aggressive behavior?" I asked. "Assault? Battery? Attempted murder?"

"Nothing he was caught for, just the stealing," Finn said. "That doesn't mean he hasn't branched out, though. He could have tried to take something from Hortense and she discovered him or confronted him when she found an item missing, so he silenced her."

"Where does he live?" I asked. "We should pay him a visit."

"He'll be at the sanctuary right now. It's one of his volunteer days. Let's see what he has to say for himself."

Finn flew, and I cast a translocation spell to get us to the sanctuary as quickly as possible.

Augustus raised a hand when he saw us marching toward him, unaware of the trouble coming his way. "I'm glad you're here. There aren't many of us in today. Where's Dawn?"

"Behind bars," Finn said. "And you'll be too if you don't tell me the truth."

Augustus almost dropped the bucket he held. "What's she done? And what's it got to do with me?"

"Why don't you tell me?" Finn's wings were flared as he stood in front of Augustus, his face flushed with rage. "You lied to me."

"About what?" Augustus adjusted his grip on the bucket and glanced our way. "I'm confused."

"Let's start with your references. You told someone to provide you with fake references so you could get a spot here."

"Oh! That. I thought that had been dealt with. I mean, not dealt with. I assumed you were happy with me, so you wouldn't pursue my referees. I can give you more names."

"I met your friend, Donnie," I said. "He was helpful. He said you met when you were imprisoned for theft."

Augustus opened his mouth, but nothing came out.

"And we know your real name," Finn said. "I've looked you up. The real you."

Augustus set down the bucket, his shoulders sagging. "That changes things. But I hope you understand now why I didn't tell you the truth. I've left all that behind, and I don't want any trouble. I crave a quiet life. A place where no one bothers me."

Finn's scowl didn't soften. "I'm not an unreasonable guy, and my door is open to people who want to turn over a new leaf, but what you did was deceitful."

"You'd most likely have gotten away with it if you'd paid Donnie what you were supposed to," I said. "He had no issue with giving you a cover story or two."

Augustus winced. "I meant to, but I was short on money, and I hoped he'd forget. It was only a small favor."

"Pretending to be someone you're not to get something you want isn't small," Finn said. "This'll get you in trouble."

"No! Please, don't send me back inside. I love it here. I know I should have told the truth, but I wasn't sure how long I was staying." Augustus gently kicked at the bucket. "I move around a lot because

I've never felt like anywhere was home, so I drift from one place to another, doing cash-in-hand jobs, keeping my head down. But when I came here, it felt different. This feels like a place I could call home."

Finn rocked back on his heels. "And what about Dawn?"

Augustus's forehead furrowed. "What about her? Why is she in a cell? Does this have to do with me faking my references? She had nothing to do with that."

"We found evidence to suggest she murdered Hortense," I said. "But we have one problem. You provided her with an alibi. Were you lying about that, too?"

Augustus took in a breath and let it out slowly. "In a way, but Dawn's not the killer."

"You'd better explain," Finn said. "Or there's a cell with your name on it."

"Please, I've had enough of living like a criminal."

"So, tell the truth," Zandra said. "What do you know about that night?"

Augustus looked around, a wistful expression on his face, suggesting he knew what he'd lose if he didn't speak up. "I don't know how, but Hortense found out I'd lied about who I was. She knew I'd served time. She confronted me when we were at the sanctuary and demanded money. She said she'd tell everyone who I was, and I'd lose what little I had if I didn't pay for her silence."

"Hortense didn't reveal your secret," Finn said. "What did you give her to keep her happy?"

"I had a small amount of savings. I've been putting a little away every week. I was thinking of buying a second-hand van and converting it so I could live in it. I was even hoping you might find room here so I could park it."

Finn nodded. "Go on."

"Hortense took it all. She said it would do for now, but she'd be back for more, and if I didn't pay, I knew the consequences." Augustus shuddered.

"That gives you an excellent motive for murder," I said.

"Yeah, and I'm aware of that," Augustus said. "Why do you think I've kept quiet?"

"How does Dawn come into this?" Finn asked.

"She must have overheard me arguing with Hortense. Dawn knew why she was blackmailing me. The night Hortense was killed, Dawn dashed over in a panic. She was sweating and shaking. She'd disappeared for about ten minutes. I don't know where she went, and she wouldn't tell me, but she begged me to give her an alibi. She said something bad was about to happen and she couldn't be involved." A gentle smile crossed Augustus's face. "She loves working here too, so I sympathized. We all know Dawn. She has this tough exterior, but she's soft-hearted. And she's not the killer."

"Are you sure?" Finn said. "Maybe she killed Hortense and then used you to cover for her."

"That's not what happened. Dawn told me she knew Hortense was in trouble and someone was unhappy with her. That someone paid Dawn to keep watch while they killed Hortense."

"Who paid Dawn?" I asked.

"I don't know! And I didn't know the plan was to murder Hortense. She was always putting people's backs up, so I assumed someone planned to rough her up to teach her a lesson. I'd never have agreed to be Dawn's alibi if I knew it would end in a death." Augustus's tone suggested he didn't believe that. Hortense had been nothing but trouble for him, so he must be relieved she was dead.

"It could still be Dawn who killed Hortense," Finn said. "She had the opportunity, and she's got a strong motive. Do you know about the illegal animal selling?"

"Err... Not a clue. I already told you that. Who's involved?" Augustus asked.

"Dawn," I said.

He shook his head. "No chance."

"We have proof. And she's confessed."

Augustus appeared genuinely shocked. "Huh! I had no idea. She wouldn't do that willingly. Did Hortense make her do it?"

"Possibly," Finn said. "What do you know?"

"I swear, nothing! It must have been Hortense's influence. She was a bad person. She scared people. Hortense even intimidated me."

Finn folded his arms. "Did you and Dawn kill Hortense together?"

"No! It wasn't me, and it wasn't Dawn. I'm telling the truth. And I trust Dawn. I doubt she'd have agreed to be involved with the killer's scheme if she knew what they had planned. The poor girl must be terrified."

She may be terrified, but we were stumped. Who paid Dawn to be the lookout while the killer acted?

"Dawn's still not talking." Finn came out of the cells and closed the door. "But Augustus was right about her being terrified. She won't stop shaking."

"Let me speak to her," I said. "Dawn loves animals, so she may open up if I'm around."

Finn glanced at Cythera's closed office door. "Go ahead. I need something solid fast, or this case will fall apart."

I entered the corridor with Zandra and Finn, and we stopped by Dawn's cell. She was curled on the cot with her arms wrapped around her knees. She looked even more fragile in that position, and her body shook.

"I'm done talking," she whispered. "You won't believe me, whatever I tell you."

"I'll believe your confession." Finn sighed. "But you need to stop holding out on us."

"Dawn, Augustus told us he gave you an alibi for the night of Hortense's murder," I said.

"He shouldn't have done that. I thought he was my friend. I was an idiot to trust him. To trust anyone. I should have known this would happen."

"Augustus didn't realize what he was getting into by giving you a fake alibi," I said.

She sniffed. "I didn't do it."

"Who did?" I asked. "Who are you covering for?"

"I can't tell you. And even if I did, you wouldn't believe me. I'm nothing, and she's..."

"Yes? Who is she? Does she have something on you?"

Dawn shook her head and stared at the floor.

"We want to get to the truth," Zandra said. "Whoever it is, they can't hurt you while you're in here."

Dawn's panicked gaze lifted to meet Zandra's. "How do you know that? They're powerful. They'll come after me if I tell you everything."

"You'd rather go to prison?" Finn asked. "You don't trust us to do the right thing?"

"I'm... not sure. Angels haven't helped me much in the past."

"Hortense may not have been the nicest of people, but she deserves justice," I said. "Preventing us from getting it won't help."

"I'm safer behind bars," Dawn mumbled. "At least I'll have a bed and get fed. I've got no support out there. No one looking out for me."

"You have me," Finn said. "You should know you can trust me. I'll help you. But you have to be honest."

"You're only saying that because you want information out of me then you'll abandon me. Everyone does."

"Finn's not like that," I said. "He's a good guy."

"He works for Angel Force. I know they're not to be trusted. They've let me down one too many times," Dawn said. "I'm not saying anything else. Leave me alone."

Finn looked at us and shrugged. We left Dawn to her melancholy and walked into the office. Cythera had just arrived with a large white box in her hands.

"I need an update on the case. Finn, you're with me." She strode into her office without glancing at me or Zandra.

I followed Finn, the sweet scent from the box intriguing me. "What have you got in there?"

Cythera thumped down the box and slumped into her seat. "Maverick insisted I bring back a box of wedding cake samples for everyone. This is the first of three tasting sessions. Why do we need to eat so much cake? Anything will do."

"I can help if you have leftovers," Finn said. "I'm starving."

"Maverick is an excellent influence on you," I said to Cythera.

She tutted. "The update, now. Have you got enough evidence to charge Dawn with Hortense's murder?"

"She's not keen on talking," Finn said. "But we uncovered her alibi is fake. She wasn't with Augustus."

"That's progress. Anything else? A confession would be useful."

"Dawn said she was paid by the killer to keep watch so they wouldn't be disturbed," I said.

Cythera looked over my head as she drummed her fingers on the desk. "Did you get a name out of her?"

"She's too scared to say more," Finn said. "Dawn doesn't trust us. She thinks that, once we get the information, we'll abandon her."

Something was knocked over in the open-plan office, and there were several shrieks. Binky bounded into Cythera's office, her fur fluffed out and her tail puffy.

"Unless this is a dire emergency, you need to control yourself." Cythera jumped to her feet.

"There's a problem at the bakery!" Binky growled at no one in particular. "Tia has had a surprise visit from health and safety."

"That's no excuse to destroy my office or upset my angels," Cythera said.

Binky ignored her and stared at me. "Someone sent in an anonymous tip about the food. The bakery's food is excellent. Why would anyone complain about it?"

"If you don't calm down and stop swishing that enormous tail, I'll forcibly eject you." Cythera strode around her desk and pointed at the door.

"I'll come with you. Save me a piece of cake." I hurried away with Binky, relieved to distance myself from Cythera's acerbic tone. Spending most of the day eating wedding cake samples hadn't sweetened her.

"I don't know how to help," Binky said. "I suggested I chase the inspector away, but Tia said it was a bad idea and would make them suspicious. What do they have to be suspicious of?"

"This unexpected visit won't be a problem. Tia maintains high standards at the bakery. Having sampled many of her treats, I know they're delicious and well-made."

"The inspector is only interested in the pasties from Mystical Morsels. She's not looking at anything else."

"The complaint must have been made about them, then. I must admit, when I ate one, it was gristly. I'd expected better quality from such a respectable company. Their advertising always boasts about their five-star reviews."

"Tia's worried. It's the first time she's gone into partnership with a big company. She hoped this would be a springboard to set up franchises. But if people from Mystical Morsels hear about this, she could lose the deal, and her dreams will be shattered." Binky growled again. "That can't happen."

We ran while we talked and stopped outside the bakery. Sure enough, there was a stern-looking woman with a tray of pasties on the counter, prodding them and cutting off samples.

"She's been doing that with all the batches of pasties," Binky said.

"Maybe someone got sick after eating one," I said. "Food poisoning?"

"I... maybe. My stomach's been upset since I've been eating them."

"How many pasties have you eaten?"

"Five or six a day. Just a snack, really. But I keep getting a gurgling gut. Maybe it's the pastry. Too much flour?"

I sat and watched the inspector for several minutes as an idea formed. Was it a coincidence that trouble had come to town at the same time Mystical Morsels made a deal with Tia? "Binky, this pasty problem calls for some research. Are you available for a kitten impossible mission?"

Her whiskers bristled and her eyes grew wide. "It does?"

I nodded. "And I need my best felines on the job. Are you in?"

Chapter 21

Pasty problem

It had taken a fair amount of persuasion before I'd convinced Finn and Zandra to join me on the kitten impossible mission. It was the first time they'd taken part in one of my more unusual adventures, but this mission needed additional support because we were going up against a giant.

A big, meat-filled pasty giant.

It was just past nine in the evening, and we'd been watching the Mystical Morsels headquarters for an hour, as the evening staff drifted home. Only the security desk was occupied by two guards, along with one corner office, which was lit. And I had a good idea who was in that corner office.

"Are you sure about this?" Finn asked for the tenth time.

"I have a tiny amount of doubt, but it's so minuscule you'd only be able to see it under a microscope," I said. "Dawn is too scared to reveal who paid her to keep watch. That means we're dealing with someone powerful. Someone with influence."

"You really think the CEO of a food company is the killer?" Zandra didn't sound convinced.

"Celeste seems so nice." Finn pulled on his bottom lip.

"Pasties mean power. I inspected Mystical Morsels financial records, and this place has a turnover of millions in profit every quarter. They won't want anything to affect the bottom line. Since Celeste is in charge of that bottom line, she must be our focus."

"For a company that makes so much money, I'd have thought their pasties would be tastier," Binky whispered. "I mean, they're edible and easy to eat, but they're not filling. I get hungry an hour after eating them and want another."

"It's the perfect junk food," I said. "No matter how much you eat, you always want more. That's how these companies get rich."

"And we get fat." Finn patted his stomach. "So, there's something dodgy going on at Mystical Morsels, and Hortense found out?"

"Hortense worked for Celeste. And the more we've discovered about Hortense, the sneakier we realize she was. She blackmailed Augustus and took his money. She manipulated Dawn and forced her to keep giving her animals, even though she was paying half the amount she promised. Hortense wasn't kind to anyone who crossed her. I wouldn't be surprised if she snooped around Celeste's office and discovered something she shouldn't."

"Something that got her killed," Zandra said. "Something about the food they make?"

"It must be. And with Hortense's track record for blackmail, I could imagine her confronting Celeste and demanding money. And it wouldn't have been a small amount. She'd have known how wealthy Celeste is."

"Hortense blackmailed the wrong person," Finn said. "And Celeste was at the sanctuary when Hortense was killed. She could have done it."

"But we need proof," I said. "Which is why we're getting into Celeste's office and stealing her mobile snow globe. She's attached to that thing. It must contain her secrets."

Finn grimaced. "I want the killer caught, but I should have waited for a search warrant."

"That would have taken too long. And the second Celeste realized your plan, she'd have tied you up with her legal team and skipped the country. She'd have taken the money with her, wiped away all evidence, and you'd have never seen her again. We need to get her to confess to what she did. This is the only solution."

"Cythera will be so mad if this goes wrong." Finn glanced over his shoulder. "It's not too late to fill her in."

"It won't go wrong because you have us here," I said. "We've watched the security guards' rotation. One of them leaves his desk every hour to patrol. The next time he goes off, we sneak in."

"But there are two of them," Binky said. "I can bite the one left behind. Pin him by the throat until you get in and out. It doesn't have to be a lethal bite. I have control."

"No biting! Finn and Binky, you tackle the lone security guard. Finn, use your angel charm. Make up a story about there being break-ins in the area and you want to know if they've seen anything. He won't be suspicious of you. While you do that, we'll go to Celeste's office. We'll wait for her to leave and then snoop around."

"Got it," Binky said. "I'll put biting into Plan B."

"Put it in Plan Z," I said. "Better still, don't have it in a plan at all. We don't want you behind bars again."

"I'd do it if it protects Tia's bakery. I can't believe she's in partnership with a killer, though. She'll be so disappointed Celeste deceived her and off-loaded shoddy products on her." Binky swished her glorious tail.

"It's better to find out now than when she's opened dozens of businesses with Mystical Morsels and the dirty truth comes tumbling out," I said.

Binky jerked her chin up. "Look! One of the security guards is on the move."

"That's our cue," I said. "Does everybody know what to do?"

The group nodded.

We crept to the entrance of the glass-fronted building. Zandra and I hung back while Finn strode in with Binky, all smiles and glistening wings. We heard Finn warmly greet the security guard then move him to one side of the desk so the guard had his back to us.

Zandra eased open the door, and we tiptoed inside, making it past the desk and around the corner, out of sight of the guard.

"The other guard should be patrolling the first floor," I whispered. "Let's use the elevator to get up to the corner penthouse. I'm certain that's where Celeste is based. The CEO always gets the best office."

We dashed to the elevator, wincing as it announced its arrival with a ping. But the security guard didn't notice and seemed deep in conversation with Finn about the fake break-ins.

The ride was smooth as we zoomed to the top floor, and luck was on our side because we only had to wait in a dark, empty room a few minutes before Celeste left her office, a mug dangling from one finger.

We dashed into the room. Clean lines and an open layout greeted us. The walls were painted in a soft, calming shade of off-white, and pictures of delicious food items were strategically placed around the room. The focal point was a sleek desk made of polished rosewood. It stood in the center, facing the windows. The desk was kept meticulously organized, with a sleek silver laptop, a wireless charging pad, and a collection of elegant stationery.

"You take her desk. I'll look around everywhere else," I said.

"We'll only have a few minutes," Zandra said. "Let's just grab her mobile snow globe and go."

"I want to see if there's anything else we're missing." I swiftly searched through several filing cabinets but found nothing of interest.

"I've got it! It was in her purse." Zandra held up the mobile snow globe.

I did a final look around the office, and then we hurried into a nearby empty room and eased the door shut.

"It's protected by a security code." Zandra frowned at the stolen snow globe.

"We need to break it open with magic," I said.

"Then she'll know we were here!"

"Celeste will know soon enough, anyway."

Zandra held the mobile snow globe between both hands. I settled my paws on top of her hand, and she blasted a spell that shimmered around the snow globe before it sprung to life.

She shook it to activate it then flipped through to the messages. She searched for Hortense's name, but nothing came up.

"Check the voice notes," I said. "There are dozens."

We listened to a few, but none were from Hortense.

"Go back further."

Zandra pressed play on an older message.

"You know who this is. And you know that I've uncovered what you're doing. You may think you've gotten away with firing me, but you made the mistake of underestimating me. Now, you're going to pay."

"That's Hortense's voice," I whispered. "She doesn't sound happy."

The voice note continued. "I'll never eat those disgusting pasties now I know the truth about their contents. And no one else will when they find out." There was a pause. "However, if you want your secret safe, I need compensation. You know how to reach me so we can make a deal. Don't take too long, or I might decide the public needs to learn the truth about Moldy Morsels and your line in dubious meat products."

"Blackmail! I knew it," I said.

The door swung open, and the lights flicked on overhead. Celeste stood in the doorway, staring at the mobile snow globe. "Is that mine?"

"Greetings! We have questions for you," I said.

"I can say the same. Were you listening to my private messages?" Celeste stepped into the room. "I'll have you arrested."

"We're doing our job and solving a crime," I said. "The crime you're in the middle of. Exactly what goes into your pasties that got Hortense so hot under the collar?"

Celeste's top lip curled a fraction then she smiled. "My apologies for being abrupt. I won't contact Angel Force. You startled me, that's all."

"I imagine the last thing you want is angels poking around and asking questions about quality control." Zandra arched an eyebrow.

Celeste took in a slow breath. "I must have dropped my snow globe in the corridor. You were listening to the messages to find out who it belonged to. Isn't that right?"

Zandra shook her head. "There's evidence on here to suggest you murdered Hortense."

Celeste lifted both hands and moved them gently back and forth. "Everything can stay the same. You found my lost snow globe, and I'm willing to compensate you. I'm so grateful you discovered it. I can barely function if I don't have it. Technology, it was supposed to set us free, but it's made slaves of us in a different way. Name your price. Whatever you want, it's yours."

"You want us to return your mobile snow globe and keep quiet about what we've discovered?" I tilted my head.

"Yes! You got it. What would you like?" Celeste smiled encouragingly at me.

"We're not being silenced with your money," Zandra said. "That's what Hortense was interested in, though. How much did she want from you?"

Celeste stepped closer, still smiling. "I can give you whatever you desire. A new house, enough money so you never need to work again. Dream vacations. Think about it before you dismiss this opportunity. It'll be for everyone's benefit."

"Not for the people who eat your dodgy food," I said.

"There's nothing dodgy about the products this company produces," Celeste said sharply. "Watch what you say or I'll have you in court for slander if you spread lies. I've done it before."

"You won't do that. Because that would make people look closely at your food, just as the health and safety inspector is doing at Tia's bakery. They're interested in your pasties." I flicked my ears up and down.

Celeste's tongue tracked across her bottom lip. "Perhaps Tia isn't storing the products correctly. This has nothing to do with Mystical Morsels."

"You're not blaming this on Tia!" Binky barged into the room, with Finn behind her.

Celeste stumbled back, magic briefly lighting up her fingers, but then she lowered her hand and sighed.

"Did you get what we needed?" Finn asked.

I nodded. "Hortense's threat to reveal everything is on Celeste's mobile snow globe. She intended to ruin this company if she didn't get her blackmail demands met."

Finn turned on Celeste. "Got anything to add?"

She met his furious glare with a calm one. "Name your price."

"Excuse me?"

"I'm wealthy and powerful. Tell me what you want to make this go away and it's yours. Money for your sanctuary? I can make it so you never have to worry about another bill. You could expand, help more animals. Wouldn't that make you happy?"

Finn's demon energy flickered around him, and he growled.

Celeste gulped. "Or a new start somewhere else. Forget the stresses of Angel Force. An island! Your own private island, where you can do... this." She waved a hand at his demon power. "And no one will bother you. I... I broke no laws!"

"Just distorted them beyond recognition and ensured no one was around to reveal the truth," I said.

Celeste ignored me. "Finn! I like you. We can be friends. Tell me what you most desire."

He bared his teeth. "For you to go to prison for the rest of your sorry life. Tell us the truth."

She lowered her head, and her body sagged. "Hortense was going to ruin everything. I'd lose this business, and hundreds of people would lose their jobs. I had to stop her. She was crazy enough to follow through with her threat."

"You stopped her by killing her, rather than giving in to her blackmail demand?" I asked.

"Hortense wouldn't have stopped. She once bragged that she had a knack for finding a person's weakness and using it for her own benefit. That was on the last date we went on. I knew then there was something wrong with her. She thrived on people's despair. If I'd accepted her blackmail proposal and paid her off, she'd never have left me alone. She'd have bled me dry and then probably revealed what we were doing out of spite."

"You're using substandard products in your food?" Finn asked. "Fillings not fit for consumption to save money and maximize profit?"

Celeste said nothing.

"We'll ask the health and safety inspector. They'll keep digging," I said. "They'll get to the truth. Then it'll go public, and this company will be finished."

Celeste sighed. "Maybe a few corners were cut, but it's still an excellent product."

"Your pasties are gristly," I said.

"And I've had an upset stomach since I started eating them," Binky said.

"This isn't my fault!" Celeste cried out. "Hortense was horrible, and she only ever looked out for herself. She deserved to be killed. The world is a better place now she's not in it."

Finn stepped forward. "And you deserve to be charged with her murder."

Chapter 22

Final rescue

"This is the spot." Finn stood by the roadside, an anxious expression on his face as he looked around. We were surrounded by woodland, a secluded area, perfect for making illegal animal exchanges without being noticed.

I stood beside Binky. We had our heads up, sniffing, trying to catch a scent of either the animals that had been taken or Hortense.

"We need something that'll lead us to those animals," Finn said. "I haven't been able to sleep, worrying about where they are."

Zandra squeezed his shoulder. "We'll find them. We've got two of the best noses here in Crimson Cove. We'll get them home."

I blocked out distractions and sniffed. Binky did the same, inhaling deeply, her top lip curled slightly as she tasted the air.

"Dawn gave us all the information she had," Zandra said. "She wants these animals found as much as we do."

Finn sighed. "She's remorseful about what she got messed up in. But she's not staying at the sanctuary. I've lost faith in her. Cythera is talking about prison, given what she's done."

"Dawn was an accomplice to murder," Zandra said. "She can't get away with that."

"And Augustus is out too." Finn scowled at the trees. "I need a win. It feels like everything is going wrong at the animal sanctuary. I'm losing volunteers, and now Celeste's been charged with murder, so the support from Mystical Morsels has vanished. Maybe this is a sign."

I paused from my intense sniffing. "It's a sign life throws us challenges. It's how we rise to meet them that's important. And you're not alone. We can work out a schedule so the sanctuary doesn't overwhelm you. Maybe you could appeal to Cythera's kind side for extra time off until you sort things."

"She has a kind side?" Zandra asked.

"She hides it well, but it's there. Now, stop talking. You're distracting us from locating relevant scents."

They fell silent, and we kept sniffing. Finn had provided an item of Hortense's clothing taken from her body, so we had a decent idea of what to smell for. We were also looking for scent trails from any stolen animals. Finn had uncovered twenty trades, so we had a lot to sniff out.

Binky tensed. Her head lifted even higher, and her tail pointed straight out behind her.

"Do you have something?" I whispered.

She nodded then bounded away. We followed as she dashed toward the trees, following a faint path that led us deeper into the woods. The trees were heavy with foliage, making it gloomy as we continued.

I inhaled deeply. "I smell Hortense too! It's faint, but I've got her."

We continued on foot for fifteen minutes until we came to a narrow dirt road. There were tire tracks in the dust.

"This road must branch off from the main road," Finn said, inspecting the tracks. "I figured Hortense wouldn't have traveled far with the animals in case she drew attention. She made the trade with Dawn then came down here. There must be a shed or storage barn nearby."

Binky had stopped tracking and was sniffing again.

I walked over to join her. "Do you sense magic? Barrier spells or concealment magic? The animals Hortense took had powers, so they'd need to be safely contained so they can't escape."

"There's something tickling my nose," she said. "What about you?"

I tuned into the fields of power around us. "This way."

We were off again, following the dirt road this time. It split into two forks, and Binky and I took the left fork. We rounded the bend, and the road stopped. To the right of the road was a small shed. It had been well concealed by foliage, but the flickers of magic in the air gave it away.

"We found them!" I yelled.

Finn appeared with Zandra and rushed toward the shed. He bounced backward and hit the dirt.

"Barrier spell." He grunted as he pulled himself to his feet.

Before we had time to offer assistance, he slammed his hands against the barrier. Flickers of his demon power spun across his wings in hot red spirals, surrounding the shed. There was a brief explosion of sparks, and the barrier disintegrated.

Finn shook his wings and rolled his shoulders, taking a moment to get his demon energy under control. He glanced back at us and nodded. "Zandra, go grab the van so we can load up the animals."

"On it." She cast a translocation spell and disappeared.

Finn strode to the door. He pulled it open and stared inside. I joined him with Binky, relieved to see the animals inside had bedding and water, although their food bowls were empty. There were squeaks and grunts as we stepped inside. Finn walked around the pens, talking gently to the animals and checking on them.

I nudged Binky with my head. "Well done. We did it."

"I wasn't gonna let that devious creature harm any of us," Binky said. "Tia is so upset by everything that happened. She's embarrassed she was fooled into a deal with a company selling dodgy meat products."

"We were all fooled," I said. "Mystical Morsels had a solid reputation. Why should she think they made poor-quality products?"

"Their reputation was built on lies." Finn was still focused on the pens. "The contact I made in health and safety said they've received dozens of complaints from an anonymous source, all about the same thing."

"The anonymous source being Hortense?" I asked.

"We can't know for certain, but it must have been her. She wrote them letters. Since Celeste decided not to bend to Hortense's blackmail demands, Hortense was determined to ruin her."

"And she succeeded, even though the cost was her life," I said. "That's what bitterness gets you. You end up alone and—"

"With a hayfork stuck in your chest and a gross pasty shoved down your throat," Binky said. "Lesson learned. Don't be a jerk."

"That's close enough," I said. "Celeste made sure the last thing Hortense tasted was the secret she intended to leak."

"But Hortense was smart as well as sneaky," Finn said. "The anonymous tip-offs were her backup plan. Even when dead, she was able to take down her nemesis. Imagine what she could have achieved if she'd been a good person."

The van rumbled to a stop outside, and a moment later, Zandra appeared. "How's everyone doing?"

"Looking good." Finn heaved a sigh. "The trouble is, I don't have room for all of them at the sanctuary. As soon as a place comes free, it's filled."

"We can help," I said. "We've got room at animal control. They can stay there temporarily. Once you've checked them over and made sure they're not traumatized, they can go on to their forever homes, can't they?"

Finn nodded. "I need to make sure there's still space for them, but I hope we can get them to where they belong as quickly as possible."

"Let's get to work," I said.

The next hour was spent loading the animals into the van, and then we were back on the road, returning to Crimson Cove. We took a few animals to Finn's sanctuary, and the rest returned to animal control. Finn came with us, but I could see he was tiring. I'd generously given him my seat in the van and spent a moment comforting him by making biscuits on his lap.

It was a tight fit because Binky was with us, too. But when we arrived, she leapt out and headed to the bakery to be with Tia and give her the good news.

Barney met us at the door of animal control. "Did you find them?"

"The mission was a success." I climbed off Finn's lap and jumped to the ground.

Barney's smile was full of relief. "I got your message, Zandra. I made room for the extras. Let me help you get them inside and settled."

Twelve of the creatures would be temporarily living at animal control. Two hardy crested bobble haired skinks could comfortably sleep in the outdoor pens, but the rest needed to be inside, so we took them to the back room where Sammy, Tinkerbell, and Ember lived.

"While I'm here, I'll look at the prisoners," Finn said. "Do my weekly check-up."

"Sammy's been on his best behavior," I said. "He always is."

"You may be biased there." Finn walked into the room and checked on them. Sammy was quiet, Tinkerbell ignored him, and Ember was chirpily happy and answered all of Finn's questions.

Barney brought in a pen and set it down. He went straight to Ember and talked softly to him after Finn had moved on.

I stood back and watched with Sammy. "I think we have a match."

"Barney's a calming influence on Ember. And he's been saying how much he likes him. Do you think they'll attempt a bond?"

"If they do, it could be the making of Ember. Barney is solid and reliable, and he's been lonely since he lost his familiar."

"Lonely enough to try to bond with me."

I huffed warm air at Sammy. "Neither of you was ready for a bond. And you'll know when you find the right one. You need to learn to trust again."

Sammy glanced at me. "We all need to do that. I'm working on it."

"Still losing your fur, I see," Tinkerbell said to me.

"I'm stress-shedding from having to deal with you. Still rude, I see."

She turned her back to me and curled into a ball.

I wasn't sure what the future held for Tinkerbell, but with Sorcha looking out for her, she'd make it through. But the journey would be rough if she kept resisting.

"Everyone looks good." Finn stepped out of the way as Zandra brought in the last pen. "Life can finally get back to normal in Crimson Cove."

I waited until Barney had left the room and the door closed. "Normal? You're forgetting you're a new father?"

Finn looked at the ceiling. "I haven't forgotten."

"You have a plan to deal with the baby?" Zandra asked. "She's cute, but you can't keep her."

"Can't I? I don't think the sanctuary is being watched anymore, so there's no threat."

I walked over to Finn and head-butted his calf. "They don't give up one of their own easily."

"They might. I'm taking each day as it comes."

"You need a plan," Zandra said. "You can't sit back and let them take control."

"I'm not. I'm working on something."

"Has Torrin been any help in finding you a solution?" I asked.

Finn raised his eyebrows. "He's not helping with that. He's got other things on his mind. I'm there as a shoulder to lean on since he's going through some stuff."

"Don't you think you have enough on your plate?" Zandra said.

Finn shoved his hands into his pockets. "It'll be fine. Won't it?"

I wasn't certain it would, but we'd solved the immediate problem. Celeste had been charged with Hortense's murder, Dawn and Augustus would be appropriately punished for their involvement, and the traded animals were back where they belonged and would soon go to a happier place.

As for Finn and his dragon hatchling, that was a problem to solve another day.

About the Author

K.E. O'Connor (Karen) is a mystery author living in the beautiful British countryside. She loves all things mystery, animals, and cake. If you want to practice spells, solve a few murders, and spend time with amazing witches and their talking familiars, join her weekly newsletter.

Sign up today

Newsletter: https://BookHip.com/GXDVFRA
Website: www.keoconnor.com/writing
Facebook: www.facebook.com/keoconnorauthor

Also By

Witch Haven: Welcome to Witch Haven, where nothing is what it seems. Meet four fabulous witches as they struggle with their destinies, deal with misfiring magic, murder, and the Magic Council.

Crypt Witches: Meet Tempest Crypt, a witch who swallows demons, and Wiggles, her mini talking hellhound, while you enjoy magical murder and intrigue.

Lorna Shadow: A cozy mystery series set in the fun world of a personal assistant who sees ghosts. Meet Lorna, her ditzy sidekick, Helen, and Flipper, the dog who senses ghosts, as they solve crimes and save the day.

Holly Holmes: An adorable cozy culinary mystery series set in the beautiful village of Audley St. Mary. Each book is full of treats, murder, and twists. Join Holly and Meatball, her clue-hunting dog, as they solve murders and eat cake.